THE QUARANTINE OF

ST. SEBASTIAN HOUSE

a novella

by John Pistelli

In Memoriam

Mary Pistelli
(1922-2020)

Nunzia DiPaolo
(1929-2020)

William Dallessandro
(1942-2020)

He has been a sick man all his life. He was always a seeker after something in the world, that is there in no satisfying measure, or not at all.

—Walter Pater,
Imaginary Portraits

1. The Land of the Deed

I didn't know my neighbors until the pandemic quarantine. We lived in the St. Sebastian House—so it said on the flaking wood lintel above the front door—an ancient three-floor red-brick apartment building overshadowed by two taller and more recent prefabricated structures in the pastel shipping-container style. We were probably slated for demolition, but we didn't know when it would come. As for the name, St. Sebastian House, I assumed but could not confirm with a simple Internet search that the building must have served as some kind of rectory or convent or sanitarium for a long-defunct church before an enterprising soul turned it to commercial purposes. Three floors, two apartments each: I lived in the right-hand rooms on the second floor. One window in front overlooked the city side-street we sat on, one window on the side was above an alley dark even in the daytime, and one window in the rear opened onto a weedy fenced-in back lot where a moss-devoured Virgin Mary topped a sunken stone birdbath. And until the quarantine, I did not know my neighbors.

I was 25 years old then. I had stayed in the city for graduate school—I'd come from the suburbs to go to the University—but St. Sebastian House was my first apartment outside of dormitories. Even before the quarantine, I didn't handle my freedom especially well. I spent the days I didn't have to teach or attend seminars in alcoholic and other forms of dissipation, avoiding my father's calls and trying not to think about where the money came from to pay for my wasted life. I cashed his checks and avoided his calls; I lived on vodka and tinned tuna; I would try to read Plato or Hegel or Simone Weil and find myself trawling the porn sites.

I always made a habit of ignoring the news, because it reminded me too much of how and why my mother died, a story I will tell in its proper place. So the announcement in early spring that a novel virus so endangered public health that the University would close its doors and "transition to online instruction," that all non-essential businesses would close, and that we were all encouraged—with encouragement to be supplanted by force should we prove noncompliant—to remain inside for some two weeks to two years caught me unawares. But how different would this quarantine be from the life I'd led in the months before that pandemic in early March? I shut myself away with my books and my booze and my tuna. Skeptical of the possibility of education in the midst of an international emergency, I converted my Introduction to Modern Philosophy class into a desultory and sparsely-attended message board. I spent hours online trying to understand the severity of the novel virus, but dueling experts, each with a different chart modeling wildly divergent outcomes based on the same data plotted different ways, convinced me that numbers were just like words: a skilled rhetorician could make them mean whatever he or she wanted them to mean. I read that those over 50 were in graver danger, and I did not call my father.

Soon my Internet research led me to the new forms of pornography the novel virus had inspired. I was watching one such video at the end of the quarantine's inaugural week when I met the first of my neighbors. Onscreen, a beautiful woman in a nurse's uniform and surgical mask informed me that the virus had almost entirely obliterated humanity and that I was in fact the last human male alive. To repopulate the planet, she would need to harvest my—

I jumped and slammed shut the laptop at the sharp metallic raps on my door: ringed fingers, knocking.

"My name is Denise," she said when I opened the door. "May I come in? I'm going out of my mind up there." I parted my lips to object, but she rustled past me in the doorway. "Oh, I know I'm old, but you don't have to worry about communicating the illness to me. We can't all live forever, can we?"

She let herself fall in a swift lithe motion onto the musty brown couch that was almost my apartment's only furniture—I had hauled it up from a mass of curbside trash my second week living there. If she was disturbed by the burst of dust that swirled around her head when she sat, she didn't let it show. She must have been six feet tall—taller than me—and she wore a necklace of opaque amber gemstones, culottes with a Byzantine print, and harem slippers turned up at the toe. Long straight hair, silver with threads of black, fell past her shoulders. I guessed she was about 70-something.

"Might I have something to drink? I know it's early, but it seems to me that pandemic times don't know day from night."

I poured her a plastic cup of cheap vodka in the kitchen and brought it out to her. She accepted it as if I'd passed her a crystal tumbler.

The bookshelf behind the couch had in the meantime attracted her attention: it was half-collapsed, chopped roughly out of wood planks, another ruin I'd pulled from a dumpster when I first moved to the city. With her ringed fingers she reached back and pulled down a volume, an old midcentury paperback I'd bought at the used bookshop around the corner. She cautiously leafed through the brittle pages and smiled to herself.

"Philosophy. I remember those days. Schopenhauer, Kierkegaard, Nietzsche, Heidegger, Sartre, Camus." She said their names fondly, as if they'd been her scampish former lovers. "I was a professor, you know."

"Oh. Of what?"

"What does it matter now? It's all"—she lifted her jeweled hands and waved them through the dust motes—"one subject, isn't it? But I retired. Was it that the students were getting stupider or was it my personality growing more brittle and unyielding with age? It must have been me. We should always be severe with ourselves and tender with others. One of these boys said that, didn't he? Which one?" She narrowed her eyes and scanned the shelf over her shoulder until she hit upon the name. "Schiller. That's the one. So nice to be entertained by a man of erudition. As I was saying, I retired. And then my— what shall I say? we weren't married—my *partner*"—she bent her fingers into scare quotes—"died, and there was no point living any longer in that big house. I have no heirs to leave it to anyway. So I sold it and most of my possessions and put the money in the bank and came to live here in the St. Sebastian House with a Holy Bible and a complete Shakespeare, for all the world as if I had gone to that desert island they're always threatening the literate with. I intended to learn to paint, I intended to volunteer at the local library, I intended to teach myself Japanese—but mostly I just waste the days fighting about politics with strangers on the Internet."

She drank down the scalding liquor in one draft.

I was still standing. She remembered the book in her lap and gently replaced it on the shelf.

"*Partner*," she scoffed, returning to an earlier theme. "As if that were the equivalent of *lover*, to say nothing of *husband* or *wife*. All these words they want us to say now. I remember when there were many fewer words, when we only did what we did. Now we have the words to replace the deeds—to make us forget there ever were such things as deeds. A nice clean world, that's what everybody wants, especially these days, with the invisible worm abroad. Not the dirty land of the deed."

She flowed to her feet—I wondered if she'd been a dancer.

"Well, I should leave you to your life, Mr.—"

I told her my name.

She laughed to herself. "I knew that, to be perfectly honest. It's on your mailbox in the entryway. Sometimes one just has an overwhelming urge to know one's neighbors. One can't bear for another second only knowing the spirits on the screen. The screen is an irresistible temptation, though, isn't it? I confess I typed your name in, to see what I could see." She fixed her eyes on mine; I had the urge to lower them to the floor, but I held her gaze. "And I was sorry—goddamned sorry—to hear about what happened to your poor mother."

I stammered out a thanks; I resisted the impulse to tell her she'd be much sorrier if she knew what really happened to my mother rather than what the media had been allowed to report. She put her hand forward, and then she thought better of it. She bowed to me instead. Without thinking, I gave her a military salute.

"No touching in pandemic times," she said in the doorway. "I wonder how long they'll pen us in this way. Quarantine, as I'm sure a scholar like yourself knows, comes from the Venetian: *quarantena*, 40 days, the time they'd restrict a ship to Venice harbor before the passengers could disembark in the old plague days. 40 days. I don't know if I can take it. I'll have to see what the Bible says. When I was your age, I was the most raving type of boy atheist. How could anyone look at all this"—again she sent a hand through the air—"and see an all-powerful and benevolent force at work? But in my old age I say call on whatever god will get you through the night."

From the doorway, I watched her glide in her slippers to the stairwell that would take her to her apartment above mine. She stopped, turned around, looked me from head to foot, tapped her chin in thought, and walked halfway back.

"Speaking as we were of Italians. If this goes on much longer, you should introduce yourself to your neighbor down below, Louise Portofino. Don't you sometimes hear the screaming of sawed metal from downstairs? Don't you sometimes smell melting steel? Ozone, oxygen—I don't know the words. I've never known how the world works—only what I thought of it. But I worry she'll go crazy down there in her smoky cellar workshop, in her gallery of souls. Not, you understand, that I've ever met her. Her name's on the mailbox, too. But *you* should meet her. Knock unannounced. A deed! As we used to do them. Pretend you're in the land of the deed."

Denise winked at me and turned away again, her necklace rattling. The hall was dim; every other light was burnt out, and had never been replaced by our inattentive landlord, whom I'd never even met—I sent my check to some kind of property management company. She sauntered slowly with her hands in her pockets, whistling a tune I didn't recognize.

After she'd disappeared into the stairwell, I suddenly thought I saw—I told myself I must have been mistaken—the door of the apartment across from mine quickly snap shut, as if my closest neighbor, whom I didn't know, had been watching me.

2. Christ of the Abyss

In the interests of the deed, I descended the dark stairwell—
more burnt-out lights—and knocked on Louise Portofino's
apartment door a week after Denise's visit. She lived on the
half-submerged bottom floor; the hallway windows were level
with the now-deserted street. I heard a sound like cymbals
crashing down a flight of stairs and a shouted but muffled
"Hold on!" The door opened about two inches; a gasp of air 20
degrees hotter than the hallway exhaled on my face. Hands in
thick gray gloves thrust a yard of copper piping out into my

sternum. I saw at the other end of it a face in a black welder's mask overspilled by long, dark, curly hair.

"No further," came the muted voice from behind the mask. "I'm working on a commission for April 15th, and I can't afford to get sick."

"I'm not sick," I said. "I've been inside for over a week. I haven't seen anybody"—a white lie, considering Denise's visit: I felt an instant inner bite of conscience, but I was sure all the same I wasn't sick. "I live upstairs. I'm sure you've heard me pacing."

A sigh hissed hotly beneath her blank black face. The strip of plastic that showed her dark eyes clouded. She shook off her left glove and said, "Put out your hand." I stretched my arm with a wince as the pipe-end pinned the skin of my chest to the bone. Her fingers—red, hot, and plump from being confined to the thick glove—sought my pulse.

"How do I know *you're* not sick?" I asked her.

"My thermometer's broken. I must have been taking my temperature too much. But I haven't seen a soul in three weeks. Anyway, tachycardia's a reliable sign of febrility. My resting heart rate is 64 beats per minute and hasn't moved in a month. What's your resting heart rate?"

"I've never had occasion to—"

She sighed again and nudged me with the pipe to silence me. Her fingers palpated my wrist until she found the flutter above my radius; she silently counted to herself, though what standard she used to measure my heartbeat I could not tell. "Seems a bit high," she concluded and dropped my hand. My own palm had begun to sweat.

"You're making me nervous," I ventured.

She reached forward and snatched my hand again, pulling me with such force into the end of the pipe that I thought my skin would tear. "One more time," she said. Close your eyes and try to think of something peaceful."

I closed my eyes, but who could think of anything peaceful? In pandemic times? It had been a week since Denise's visit, two weeks since the quarantine officially began. I had dutifully stayed in my apartment—with two exceptions— before my visit to Louise. How much longer could I stay? I was never one who needed intimate company, but the continuity of ordinary life that I saw in crowded cafés, libraries, and university buildings prevented anxious memories from overthrowing my mind. There was no such protection against one's own ravening psyche under quarantine.

News of the novel virus remained terrifying but inconclusive. 80% of the population would inevitably become infected, warned some experts, while others insisted that an epidemiological law of diminishing returns would cause the malady to exhaust itself before it had afflicted any but a minuscule number, in which case the economic collapse and civil disorder portended by the quarantine would prove to have been in vain. But even that best-case scenario might strain health-care provision and endanger the most vulnerable, so extraordinary measures would have to continue. Some said the virus came and went like a bad chest cold; some said it permanently calcified the lungs, petrified the heart, abraded the spine, insulted the liver, and lacerated the very organs of generation.

There was no sorting fact from fabrication online, no discriminating between the unbelievable but true rumor and the merely plausible hoax. Martial law was coming, some said

—some even spelled it right. Soon the police—or, still worse, the military—would shoot to kill if they saw any citizen abroad without a surgical mask. Soon men in hazmat suits would be cramming the feverish, as their screams burbled through blood-foam coughs, into the Black Marias, never to be seen again. There would inevitably be a vaccine, some promised—and a digitally implanted certificate to go with it, the eyes of the state and of the corporate monopolies blinking forever in your epidermis. We would see tank treads crack the stones of the avenues; we would see stadia requisitioned just to hold the massing dead. No traffic bothered the streets, so I could hear in those warm, humid, early-spring days the returned birds sing at all hours. Yes, my heart rate was elevated.

The night of Denise's visit, I came awake with the feeling of a hand at my throat. Had the novel virus's signature shortness of breath come for me at last? Or was it just a congestion in my chest of perturbations contracted from the Internet? I stood gasping and hacking and then walked without thought straight out of my apartment, down to the front entryway, and out the door. I let it slam behind me. Who cared who heard?

The absent landlord had mounted a black glass nipple meant to suggest a camera in the corner of the entryway ceiling, but I suspected it was a fake, a surveillance-age scarecrow to ward off the credulous burglar. Criminals, I'm sure the landlord had read somewhere, are a cowardly and superstitious lot. The time must have been three in the morning. The sidewalk was chilled with drizzle and dew. I stood in my socks and boxer shorts, but who was there to notice or deride? I decided that, to calm myself, I would circle the building once, just to pace a larger perimeter than my apartment's.

I had almost completed this circuit—I'd passed the Virgin Mary and come three quarters of the way down the alley—when I saw a fiery light flash into the dark. It lit up the detritus, the piled recyclables and uncollected garbage bags. The flame flared with a scorching crackle behind the small open window of the basement apartment. I warily stepped closer, walking between the glass shards and strewn pebbles the hellish light disclosed. As I approached the window, a jet of acrid metallic smoke belched out to blind and choke me. I didn't want to be heard—in pandemic times—coughing in the street, so I ran as quickly and as quietly as I could back to my own apartment. Did I see Denise smoking a clove cigarette on the front stoop or did I dream her in my blindness? Did I hear her say, "Taking the air?"

I shut my apartment door behind me. I flushed my eyes and tried to expectorate into a dirty towel as I tasted the fumes—like burning coins—from the alley in the back of my throat. I thought I heard from below the bathroom floor a sound like the one you hear when you press shut the flaps of your ears. I remembered Denise's words about a "smoky workshop" and finally googled Louise Portofino. Or, as her website had it, *Louise Portofino: Sculptor in Steel.*

Still, I didn't visit her. I still didn't take my father's calls. The longer I didn't answer, the more unimaginable it became to begin speaking to him again. I read about viral loads, comorbidities, the rumored movement of armored tanks. I watched videos of distant hospitals where patients gasped in crowded corridors; I watched videos where women offered to cure me of my novel virus by unspeakable means.

Days later, I left my apartment again—dressed this time, even showered and shaved. I walked upstairs to visit Denise, just for the sound of a real human voice, and perhaps to learn more about sculpting in steel. Instead I was waylaid by Denise's next-door neighbor. As I passed, he opened his door to drop a full garbage bag into the hallway.

"Hey, man," he said, "don't you live downstairs?" I told him I did. He said, "Come on in here for a minute."

I squinted warily at him: he looked unwell, if not exactly sick. In the low light he appeared sallow and overweight, with thin hair on top and bushy graying curls to the side. He wore thick, square, yellowish glasses and a soiled T-shirt that bore the image of Maria the Robot from Fritz Lang's *Metropolis*. He bowed to me with his palms pressed together at his chest—the handshake had truly gone extinct, one of the novel virus's first victims—and said, "I'm Justin Appleton. I'm the projectionist at the Royal Cinema around the corner." He must have led with this to explain the state of his apartment as he led me inside: cascades of what had once been orderly stacks of DVDs spilled across the floor. A rumpled, deflated, jaundiced mattress sat at the center of the room; a giant TV monitor too big to be mounted to the wall precariously slanted against it instead.

Without embarrassment, but with no grace to his heavy movements, Appleton clambered over the mattress to collect the dirty paper plates scattered at its edges. The room smelled of sweat, marijuana, and frozen dinners. *Andrei Rublev* flickered on the giant screen; politely averting my eyes as Appleton tidied up, I tried to see if the film had gotten to the part where they kill the horse, the only part I could remember. I wondered if I could rightly ask him whether or not the theater would be going out of business due to the quarantine. What small enterprise could continue operating for weeks and weeks without any profit?

Either Appleton had telepathy or we had little else to discuss, because he said, "Don't worry about the Royal, man —we're staying open no matter what. My father finally died last year, and I sold the house. I was going to finance my first film with the money—I've been writing the script for 10 years"—he gestured to a card table in the corner sagging under the weight of a laptop and a pile of library books—"but now I guess I'm using it to keep the theater open. No point making a movie if there are no theaters."

"What's your script about?"

"It's an adaptation of the Gospel of Thomas." He smiled conspiratorially as if I would naturally join him in relishing the scandal of this concept.

He shuffled in his socks to the kitchen to throw his paper plates away, dropping them as he went. "Do you like movies?" he called over his shoulder.

I couldn't just then think of a persuasive answer. On the one hand, who didn't like movies? Who would say *no* to such a question, and in the face of a man who had devoted his life to the art? On the other hand, I much preferred reading; I found my imagination enlivened by having to conjure images from words for myself, and I liked being able to control the pace of my own experience rather than having some impersonal apparatus dictate to my docile attention. My somewhat desperate reliance for pleasure on pornographic videos just proved the imaginative poverty to which I'd been sunk since my late teen years.

Appleton did not in any case wait for my reply. He answered himself with panting excitement; he came back into the room and jerkily sawed the air with his hands.

"We can't lose cinema, man. We were already going to lose it to home streaming, but this pandemic's going to kill it off for good. And then we'll be the first society in the history of the planet that sets aside no place to come together in the flesh and deliberate over a drama or let ourselves feel awe together in the presence of a myth. The 20th century! Cinema! It was the triumph, the fulfillment of all art—a collective dream in light and sound. It made the churches obsolete. Don't you think it's everything Aeschylus and Sophocles would have wanted? The highest art. A real theophany. Humanity at prayer. And we're going to lose it, man? No way. So the Royal is staying open, plague or shine."

He couldn't suppress a smile of self-congratulation at that last line, and I chuckled with him. His speech had exhausted him. He dropped to the mattress and splayed his heavy, hairy legs in their elastic gym shorts. I remained standing. Onscreen, it was snowing in medieval Russia; Appleton and I shimmered in white light.

Though we were apparently alone, he dropped his voice to whisper: "But the reason I asked you to come in"— he looked over both shoulders theatrically—"is that we're actually still

21

open. Secret late-night screenings. It's only triple the regular ticket price—pay on the website. It'll show up as a gift certificate in case *they*"—he jerked his thumb obscurely toward the window—"are watching. Invitation only. Staggered entrance, once guest at a time. No crowding. Quarantine seating, I promise: four seats between each guest. Tomorrow night. Or morning. Three A.M. What do you say?"

"What are you showing?"

He waved his hand as if I'd asked the stupidest question in the world. "You'll find out when you get there. You don't read the priest's sermon before you go to church, do you?"

I hadn't been in a church since my mother's funeral. "Can I bring a guest?"

"As long as we get the money. Remember, man: we can't lose cinema."

So I abandoned my visit to Denise, and the next day I went to knock on Louise Portofino's door with an innocent and impersonal invitation to the cinema. She finally let my wrist fall from her hot fingers and said, "You're okay. Under 100. Probably won't kill me. Or whatever—I can die if I have to, but not before I finish this commission." She lowered the copper pipe from my breastbone.

I opened my eyes. The first thing I saw, floating in the dim distance above her black welder's mask and mass of black curls, was a poster taped to her apartment's far wall. It showed a submerged statue of Jesus: he hung in a cool blue haze. A shoal of fish drifted past, and he raised his arms to bless them. Louise followed my eyes and answered the question I didn't ask.

"*Christ of the Abyss*. They put the first one in my namesake fishing village in Italy. A sculpture—an underwater bronze— of Christ beatifying the underworld. Even as the barnacles gather and the salt eats the metal."

"You believe in Jesus Christ?"

"I believe a good sculpture can consecrate any place imaginable. I'd like one of mine on the moon." The mask smothered her voice, made it breathless and husky and deep, as if she were a militant baffling her tone and timbre as she made her demands of the world on camera. "What brings you here?" she asked.

"I just came to relay an invitation from your neighbor, Justin Appleton, on the top floor. Would you like to go to the movies at three in the morning tonight—or, I guess, tomorrow?"

"In pandemic times?"

"He promises that all necessary quarantine rules will be observed."

She raised her mask at last. I tried to read her dark face, her wide dark eyes.

"What's playing?" she asked.

At three A.M. that night or the next morning she sat four seats from me in the theater. She came in after me; she still wore the welder's mask—now to protect herself from viral miasma, the recommended masks having long ago sold out— a black jacket, and a long black skirt. She raised the mask when she sat down, and she smiled in my direction. Denise sat in the row behind us and smiled still more broadly. The seats we weren't allowed to occupy for the pandemic's sake were marked in phosphorescent blue-green paint so that even in the dark, before the film started, the theater shone with an undersea haze.

On my way in, I'd walked up a strange staircase and stolen a glance at Appleton in the projection booth. Taking no notice of me, he was threading the film from its spool into the machine to be irradiated by the xenon arc lamp. None of his movements looked awkward then; his whole body had flowed in concert with his obsolete medium, as if he were a master of the dance.

He understood we needed levity in pandemic times; he understood we needed to see our fear of being fed like the film into some impersonal machine—biological or governmental—represented and allayed; he understood we needed some innocent eros. He screened *Modern Times*, and together we laughed uneasily as the machinery manipulated the man, and together we held our collective breath as the much-put-upon hero skirted on skates at the edge of an abyss, and behind us Denise quietly sang the words to the wordless closing number: *Smile, though your heart is breaking...*

When the show ended, we crept in a staggered, slow procession back to the St. Sebastian House around the corner. Keeping 10 feet between us, we exchanged mischievous smiles. We passed the little college neighborhood's businesses and read their doom in the streetlight glare. The bookstore where I'd spend an hour or two a week browsing had a sign in the window: *Closed indefinitely — thanks for 35 years!* The tattoo shop had no announcement, but its artists had barred the door with a plank. A chain café still allowed *grab'n'go*, as they brightly advertised, but the worker-owned vegan coffee shop across the street had already gone under. The Korean grocer might have stayed open as an essential business—food provision—but thugs, having heard vaguely that the novel virus arrived from points east, had hurled stones through its windows, though I doubt they could have located any eastern countries, or western, on a map. Dawn was still a few hours away.

Almost all the St. Sebastian House's residents had attended the film screening. But who, I suddenly wondered, lived in the apartment across from Louise Portofino? And did I see in the lamplit front window of the apartment across from mine a hunched and resentful silhouette enviously eyeing our illicit excursion?

3. The Critique of Everything

He knocked like a police officer or a soldier: three hard raps on the door with the side of his fist. When I didn't answer right away, because I was spending a rare moment filming a message for my online class—a few students had emailed to complain about my lack of engagement—he pounded three times again. This startled me enough that I rose without turning off the laptop camera; I left the computer open and facing the couch on my trash-scavenged coffee table. I could hardly bring myself to open the door—Louise would have registered febrility in my pulse at this pummeling on the door.

Were the round-ups the Internet warned us about beginning at last? Or had my father grown tired of being ignored? Had he sent some of his friends in intelligence to carry me back to the suburbs?

No—the person standing at the door was only my neighbor from across the hall. He introduced himself as Arthur Brand and neither shook my hand nor bowed. He had hair so blond it appeared white; he wore it short on the sides and long enough on top that flaps of it kept flopping into his eyes. He'd brush it aside with his long, tapered fingers, and it would swing straight back. His eyes themselves were pale and red-rimmed and redly-webbed with bloody capillaries. He had belted his white button-down tightly into his tan pants, but it all seemed like it might slip at any second from his emaciated frame. He must have bought the clothes when he was a more substantial man. His cheekbones jutted with such force that I thought they might split the bloodless white skin of his face. I wished Louise Portofino were there to take his pulse; I could never rouse myself in time to do anything necessary, though, not even in my own defense. I invited him inside.

He stood inside the door, put his hands on his rawboned hips, and slowly swiveled his head from side to side on his long vein-strung neck to survey my apartment.

"From my window, it looked like a party last night," he said with a suspicious smile. "And in pandemic times!"

"We were safe," I offered. "Besides, there's not an official lock-down order yet—" I cut myself off. Was that even true? I couldn't think of any explanation that would not sound absurd. Luckily, he was only offended that no one had asked him to come.

"You can't live forever, neighbor" he said. "And I'm starting to lose it in there. Oh, I was having fun at first. A lot of fun. But even putting aside the hammering and smoke and squealing metal from my downstairs neighbor, who must be running a foundry in the cellar—"

He began to pace the apartment. The heavy heels of his scuffed black Oxfords, which he wore without socks, thundered on the bare floorboards.

"—I thought to myself when it all started that this would be the best year of my life."

He bent to my bookshelf and touched with a tapered forefinger each spine in succession, just as Louise had counted my pulses.

"Almost since I became humanly conscious—if I *am* in fact humanly conscious—I have been working in whatever way I could to undermine this country's social order."

He straightened, unimpressed with my library. I followed his booming steps into the tiny kitchen at the back of the apartment.

"When I was a little boy, my mother took me one Thanksgiving to serve dinner to what they used to call the needy. They call them something else now, to make their troubles seem less real to the educated middle classes. I call them the poor, the cursed, the wretched, the damned. The refuse of a society that, like every society at least since the institution of agriculture, requires that some starve while others eat."

He wrenched opened the sticky refrigerator door and found only condiments inside. He opened the freezer, undefrosted, thick-furred with fuzzy snow, and pried a desiccated-looking ice cube from a tray I believe the tenant before me had left. He sucked it therapeutically in his hollow cheeks.

"Forgive me for descending to rhetoric just now, neighbor. It's a useless habit. There is no one to move or persuade, no one to set things right. Just us, the ones who ruined everything in the first place."

He stood at the window and stared over the sunken Blessed Mother, shawled in moss. The ice cube yawed and squealed before it shattered in his jaws.

"That Thanksgiving was the first time I had seen the poor—really *seen* them, not just considered them as some abstract ethical concept, the people who had no dinner for whose theoretical sake I was compelled to eat my peas and greens. What I saw: the ragged hair and mottled skin, the yellowed eyes, the untreated goiter bulging in the neck, the uncleansible fingernails, the clothes worn so often they came away in flakes, the gaping mouths and black teeth, the crusted toes coming out of broken shoes, the sickly mix of bloat and starvation, the smells of mold and urine and smoke and sweat and the grease of hair. Until that Thanksgiving, I had only seen my family and their friends: Polo shirts and lawn tennis and summers at the Vineyard. And because I didn't know then about the reality of the needy, I hadn't really seen my family and their friends—I hadn't seen what made their lives possible, or what their lives made impossible. It still makes me sick to confess it. The needy looked like a different species: a realer species, the substance of which the Brands were only the shadow. We were lies projected on a wall to dazzle observers into believing the world was somehow justified despite its superabundance of agony. So instead of listening to my mother when she advised me to count my blessings and give thanks, I'm afraid I catechized *her* that night. Why were the needy needy? Why couldn't we, who had so much, simply give them what they needed? Why did I sleep in a warm bed, between smooth sheets, and they on cement in alleyways? Don't let the banality of the questions mask their urgency, please, not unless you have an answer. Well, what could my poor mother, society matron and hostess as she was, say to me?"

I stared at the side of Brand's face, trying to decide his age. Was he 30? 60?

"She must have said some variation on *it's just the way things are, God made it like this, you can't change human nature—* you know the song, I'm sure. And I was child, anyway, incapable of understanding any real answer she might have given could she have provided one, an answer that would begin, as I said, with the invention of agriculture, the institution of currency, double-entry bookkeeping, the growth of resource-extractive empires, and so on. The point is, I had seen what I had seen, and I could not unsee it. The needy would shuffle across my closed eyelids, coughing and wheezing and asking me for a dollar, so that I couldn't sleep for the racket. If I tried to eat, some image of their imposed decrepitude interposed itself between me and the food so that I could barely choke it down without retching. I resorted to prayer and superstition. Though reared in mild Protestantism, I independently evolved what my forebears, vomiting over the sides of the *Arbella*, would have regarded as popish barbarism, which just goes to show that all possible beliefs and practices are latent in every consciousness, just waiting to be summoned in an emergency of the soul. In secret, I tore at my flesh. With a ballpoint pen, I made a wound in my inner thigh, just below the groin, and kept it open for almost a year, a year of stealing towels from the laundry room to sleep on to stanch the blood. I offered the pain every night to God if only He would lift some equivalent agony from my needy brothers and sisters. My blood in return for a sufferer to have a hot meal or a sudden windfall. I had no way of knowing if God would provide; this was the mystery of faith."

He put his fingers to his temples as if to keep the veins from bursting as they pulsed visibly under the skin. He touched his forehead to the glass of the window and shut his eyes.

"My self-mortification caused a hectic blood infection that almost killed me on Christmas Eve of my 10th year, an only half-inadvertent suicide attempt and not, alas, the last. I still lay feverish in my hospital bed when my poor mother and father—who had, as they several times reminded me, given me anything any child could ever want—summoned a professional. A child psychologist. Dr. Celeste—the combination of a professional title with a first name perfect for her syrupy coercions. She was my first real glimpse at the impersonal evil that sustains, by indifference and evasion, a society brutal in its automatic functioning rather than by anyone's overtly, consciously vicious design, a society that says to its victims not *I take pleasure in destroying you* and not even *that's just the way it is* but *isn't it better this way, all things considered?* I saw her for a year as she tried to cure me of my excess care by an excavation of my deepest feelings. That the problem was out there, not in here, never seemed to have occurred to her. Dr. Celeste exhibited that style of cruel compassion, of cunning concern, in which women of a certain class seem to excel. *Do you think you're helping people by hurting yourself?* she asked. Well, that *is* what I thought, and perhaps in point of empirical fact I was mistaken, but I had the right idea. Only the liquidation of the privileged—which I had tried to accomplish literally by stabbing at my flesh—could effect the salvation of the oppressed. She tried to refer my cares to reality so that reality could disconfirm them. But facts were not the point, and her idea of reality stopped short at the boundaries of her suburban neighborhood, her suburban consciousness. The point—how could I at 11 years old explain such a thing to this well-fed woman whose fat husband played golf with my father?—the point was that if certain things were wrong then everything was wrong. And if everything was wrong, then what did it matter if I hurt myself, or, rather, how could I decently refrain from taking my portion of the pain? To some people—most especially to suburban matrons—you can't explain anything, so I simply started lying to Dr. Celeste, and she was in what must have been a rare instance happier to pronounce me cured than to continue collecting my parents' money. In retrospect, I think she must have been afraid of me. I was relieved not to have to return ever again to her office, with its bright couch and its desk teeming with commercial dolls and stuffed animals and all sorts of meaningless toys—we used them to act out our precious little feelings, Dr. Celeste and I, like the Little Golden Book of Freud's clinic."

He lifted his head and turned around; he started to fall but caught himself dizzily on the table's edge.

"It's just that I haven't eaten, neighbor" he said by way of apology.

I offered him one of my cans of tuna from the cabinet, but he waved me off.

"In pandemic times we must all tend to our own quarantine hoard. *Sauve qui peut.* That's how it is in non-pandemic times, too, but the pandemic gives us a welcome opportunity not to lie to ourselves or one another about it."

He smiled; the pale gums were coming away from his bright teeth. I followed him again as he marched out of the kitchen and stood again before my bookshelf.

"Let me abbreviate this tedious *bildungsroman* by hastening over the more hackneyed bits. I turned 12 and stopped talking to God. I began to seek the questions I had put to my benighted mother in books. I went to an elite private high school and to an Ivy League university. I read *this*"—he put his fingertip on the top corner of Plato's *Republic* and flipped it off the shelf onto the floor—"and *this* and *this* and *this* and *this* and *this* and *this* and *this*."

With each "this" he spun and flipped another book down— from Aristotle to Žižek—until he'd made a pile at his feet. Below, Louise must have wondered what was going on to create such thunder. All that remained on the shelf, all he'd left untouched, all he hadn't read, were a few novels.

"And I found any number of facts, but no answers. And the theories were worse than the facts. Every philosopher worked some apology for oppression or poverty into his system. The best philosophers were your Platos or Nietzsches, who defended domination or brutality outright. The worst were your Rousseaus or Hegels, who simply renamed evil as good or cheerfully explained why you had it coming. History was to blame. Even Marx, with his scientific theories of exploitation and dialectical justification for all that had gone before—what was he but another boy bargaining with God in the night? So I developed my own theory."

He sat down dizzily on the back of the couch; its wooden beams, beneath the threadbare upholstery, creaked a protest despite his thinness.

"If the social order generated evil out of itself because of its fundamental premise that some must have more than others, that some could get away with abusing others, then any increase in disorder prepared the way for the unimaginably just society on the other side of destruction. An unpleasant corollary to this theory was that any increase in happiness would only work to sustain the corrupt social order by making it appear better than it was. This led me to give up any dream I ever had of helping anyone, of reducing any other human being's suffering. The only kindness was cruelty.

I would never be kind again. I may have lapsed from this strict doctrine a time or two, and believe me, I regret it."

He smiled and fell over the back of my couch; then he torsioned his skeletal frame on the sagging cushions till he was nearly sitting upright.

"So I led a life of outward respectability. I lied to you earlier when I said I didn't know what the needy now were called by the middle-class engineers of language and custodians of inequality. I have worked since I graduated from the university as a grant-writer for non-profits—a job my mother, who had me destined for the law or a Senate seat, thinks is beneath me—and I can tell you every polite name we use to blunt our conscience and evade reality. We say *vulnerable populations*, we say *income inequality*, we say *food insecure*, we say *unhoused*—as if anything at all anyone could say would remove one gram of agony from this earth. And all that time I've been churning out documents to solicit meager aid from the rich and powerful, from men and women as banally self-satisfied as my mother and father. But I have also been diverting funds in secret to whoever might increase the world's disorder. Not terrorists, you understand—that's too literal. And terrorism, not unlike pandemic disease, only gives the forces of order an excuse to tighten their grip. But hackers and destroyers of property, troll brigades and agents provocateurs? Drunks in the street who will only spend what you give them on more booze and meth? All can count on my support. It's small, but it adds up. Or rather, subtracts from the vast iron prison that sits on top of us, that crushes us under—subtracts as a stream wears down a mountain."

He closed his eyes and pressed his tapered fingertips to them—just what the public health authorities warned us not to do in pandemic times. I contemplated the meagerness of his transgressions when weighed against the ferocity of his confession. When he didn't say anything for a minute, I wondered if he'd fallen asleep. But he went on, without opening his eyes.

"When the novel virus emerged, I almost danced the old hornpipe, like the festive maypole cast-outs of my ancestors' severe utopia. Here was nature to finish the job I was too squeamish to do. To cleanse the earth of our corrupt institutions and either force us to start again or wipe our failure from the universe's memory. Do you know air pollution in Southern California has gone down to nothing? That water is running blue and clear in the canals of Venice? That coyotes are loping down the streets of Chicago? If the death toll mounts high enough, the city's domestic dogs, abandoned by their deceased owners, will form packs and inherit it, parcel by jaw-reclaimed parcel. In the last week, though, my spirits have grown depressed. Doesn't it feel as if we've turned a corner? The news is all social control—governments and corporations using this crisis as their excuse to bind us ever more tightly to the knot of injustice known as our civilization. Why go on living? Some days I think it might be more preferable to step outside and lick the viral sidewalk."

He opened his eyes and found himself staring into the green light on the laptop camera and then at his own face on the screen.

"You're filming me, neighbor? Are you a cinephile, like our upstairs neighbor? Or just a pervert?"

"I'm teaching an online class. Introduction to Modern Philosophy. I was recording a message for my students when you came in and must have forgotten to stop the video."

"How educational," he said.

He took the laptop in both hands and brought it so close to his face that it captured only an indistinct impression of his pale and ruddy eyes.

"Listen, class, I'm sure if you've been listening, you must have some questions. For example, you might ask, *How can you know, Mr. Brand, that the world is unjust without some absolute standard to compare it to? In other words, doesn't your critique of Marx redound on yourself? Aren't you still just crying out to God after all these years?* Well, class, if I could answer that one—"

"I have a question," I said. I folded my arms across my chest; like the sudden onset of flu symptoms, a total and contemptuous boredom with his at-first-impressive performance settled on me. Denise, Appleton, Brand—all but Louise—I was sick of being the prey of these grand talkers. "Why did you come here to tell me all this?"

He set the laptop not back on the coffee table but at his feet and carelessly kicked it shut with the heavy heel of his Oxford. He smiled at me with only one side of his mouth.

"I was content to be alone," he said. "But I had a visit yesterday from a nice old lady who lives upstairs, and we had a nice old chat about all of you citizens of St. Sebastian House —the projectionist, the sculptress, and you. We talked, indiscreetly I think, about where your money comes from. This made me think that you of all people might sympathize with my dilemma. More than sympathize. Two sons of privilege with a war to wage on the world."

I opened the door of my apartment and stood against the jamb. Brand didn't receive the message, or silently received it and just as silently refused it: he remained sitting and smiling.

"I've never been at war with anyone in my life," I said.

4. Scraps of Steel

Quarantine may not be the right word. We learned a lot of new vocabulary in those days and used much of it imprecisely. The messages we received from higher authorities were likewise ambiguous. On some days, the president, the governor, and the mayor made separate and contradictory recommendations. Divergent schools of thought contended over the public-health benefits of legally-enforced lockdowns vs. the economic calamity that would follow from effectively stopping all business for months. Some volunteered to die for the sake of low unemployment numbers and bullish commodity markets. The scientists had not yet agreed about whether the novel virus was contracted from surfaces or from the air. It can live for years on fabric; it dies in seconds on copper; whatever you do, don't touch your face. The asymptomatic are the superspreaders; measure febrility at every door and shun the congested. At first we thought it killed only the old; then it turned out anyone with lungs and a heart was marked. The death rate fluctuated from lower than that of the common flu—if you presupposed widespread public asymptomatic infection—to more fatal than bubonic plague—if you assumed an unbroken exponential curve. The afflicted were said by some to recover, and then to fall dead a week later, twitching, in the streets. Measure per capita; extend the y-axis; focus on the rate, not the absolute number; no, the reverse. In cities without lockdown orders, public shame enforced social avoidance. But when no two scientists or politicians could agree on the most basic facts of the case— not to mention the million rumors and suppositions that scrolled by per second onscreen—what public even existed to shame? We were each our own public, each faithful to our own moral standards and passels of fact. "This is America," somebody said, "and we'll get through this the way we get through everything else: *on our own*."

By the third week, we dreamed of escape. We had all gone once more—even Arthur Brand this time—to the Royal Cinema for a three A.M. showing of *Pauline à la plage*, but when would we see the real sun again? "More like *à la plague*," Denise morosely quipped at the back of the theater.

Then Louise Portofino slipped the invitations under our doors. Sitting on the couch, I saw the white square blow over the floorboards. I opened my door a crack to see her walking the dim, crooked hallway like some post-apocalyptic plague doctor in welder's mask, inflammable gloves, corduroy overalls, and factory-grade work boots. She'd handwritten the invitations—not in cursive but in a sketchy, attenuated engineer's printing, grid-paper chirography grown languid, aslant to suggest italics.

dear neighbor

you are cordially invited to

SCRAPS OF STEEL

a premier sculptural event

by louise portofino

april 1 | 7:00pm

one-time only

masks and gloves

will be served

for pandemic times

She served the masks and gloves in front of her apartment door from an old tarnished aluminum dining tray—"It was my grandmother's," she said—embossed with grape and vine and horn of plenty. One blue surgical mask and one pair of sheer latex gloves for each of us, so we could enjoy one another's company, the citizens of the St. Sebastian House brought together at last. She, by contrast, wore a black mask and black gloves, both like silk, and a black evening dress baring her freckled pale brown shoulders, and black heels that lifted her a head higher than me. If I didn't know she was Louise Portofino, I wouldn't have recognized her.

When I arrived, she was already talking to Arthur Brand. She leaned against her closed door, bare wings of her shoulders pressed to the old wood, as she held the tray before her, her face half turned away from his own; he stood hunched in white shirt and tan pants, arms crossed, tapping

47

his sockless foot in his heavy Oxford. Was she bored or languidly seduced? Was he angry? Or was he what they called —whatever it meant exactly—smoldering?

She extended the tray to me and I masked my lower face while they continued to talk.

Brand said, "Well, Hegel said—"

"Hegel said, Hegel said," she mocked. "Hegel said sculpture belonged to the classical period and represented its perfect interpenetration of the universal and the singular—the concrete embodiment of the idea. Hegel said Christianity broke this unity by severing spirit from sense. And then Hegel said that modern art, in consequence, was devoted not to universal ideas but to subjective experience, best captured in poetry, the last stop before philosophy turned subjectivity inside out again and expressed the idea in all its glory at last, making art as such, but probably especially sculpture, completely obsolete. Yes, Hegel said all that—I went to college too, you know!—but I bet Hegel never used an arc welder."

Brand threw his arms out in frustration and turned his red-rimmed eyes and wasted cheekbones above his mask to me: "You're a philosopher—what do you think?"

"Yes, what do you think?" Louise asked. "And don't be polite. You can tell me if you think sculpture belongs in the proverbial dustbin of history before I show you my life's work."

I opened my mouth to regurgitate Camus's not unimpeachable critique of how Hegel's historicism—his dissolution of truth, goodness, and beauty into their contingent meanings at various historical stages and his consequent suspension of judgment until the acquisition on some receding temporal horizon of absolute consciousness—necessarily condemned us all to the kind of paradoxical but deadly utopian relativism that made the likes of Stalin not only possible but inevitable. In which case, I would have concluded, more for Louise's honor than out of my own personal conviction, that we had better keep an open mind about the continued viability of sculpture as an art form. I was luckily saved from this exhausting and self-serving utterance by the arrival of Denise and Appleton.

They walked together: Denise leaned on his crooked elbow, as if she were going to give him away at his wedding. Despite her long-sleeved black floral dress and her beaded black flats and her layered necklaces, she looked frailer than she had the last time I'd seen her: a slight catch was visible in her step, a slight tremor afflicted her head. Appleton—now in a button-down shirt over blue jeans, what passed for him with formal wear—took a mask from Louise's tray and tenderly affixed it to Denise's face. She held his wrists as he did so.

"Where did you get these?" Appleton asked Louise. "I heard they're going for 100 bucks apiece on the Internet."

"I have a hospital connection. You'll see."

"*Give a man a mask, and he will tell you the truth*," Denise said in her mask-muffled voice as Appleton helped her to glove her slightly tremulous hands.

"Mark Twain?" Appleton proposed.

"Oscar Wilde," Louise and I corrected in inadvertent unison. She winked at me; I returned a military salute.

"And here I thought it was Abraham Lincoln," said Brand with bitter impatience in his voice, as if he found us unutterably tedious.

In our masks, we sounded like divers in old-time metal helmets calling stifled, sweaty, breathy messages to one another at the bottom of the ocean.

"Much as I appreciate the stained plaster ceiling, the brown and extinguished lightbulbs, the threadbare carpet, and the rather slanted floor of this hallway, dear, might I ask if you'll invite us in?"

"We're not going to my apartment, Denise. We're going to my studio."

Louise pointed to the apartment across from her own. She dropped the empty serving tray with a clatter to the floor, and model-walked in her heels to the door that opened on the empty rooms from which I'd seen fire flare out into the night. We followed her inside.

The apartment was built to the same blueprint as the rest of ours—a large living room in the middle, with a bedroom and bathroom at the front of the building and a kitchen in the back. But we might as well have walked into another world entirely. The living room was as crowded as if she'd thrown a party—we hardly had space to enter—but the guests stood in unfestive attitudes.

When I walked into the room, the figure to my right sunk halfway to its knees with a baby raised in its arms—whether it lifted the child in gratitude and exaltation, or whether it

51

implored me to save the child, I could not tell. In front of me, someone tried to dance, or to catch itself as it fell, its arms held limply out, one leg drawn up like a bird's, its head tossed in broken-necked abandon or collapse. Another held its hands to its face and threw its torso back in rapture or agony. One more crawled on all fours, a supine baby facing the opposite direction beneath it, the baby's hands reaching feebly or playfully up toward its concave belly and pendant dugs. Was this a game or a disaster? A tattered and stained old couch held the center of the room. A figure had fallen onto the torn cushions, one leg on the floor, one leg thrown wildly over the back, its head lolling 45 degrees off the armrest. Another figure knelt astride the fallen one, spine arched, fists balled in the air above the other's chest. In which act of love had we surprised them—fornication or resuscitation? All together we saw 15 or 20 life-sized figures caught in postures that might have been anguish and desperation and disintegration, on the one hand, or, on the other, joy, bliss, and apotheosis.

We wandered this gallery—it smelled of burning metal—for some time; we paced and circled the figures to appreciate the various pictures they created when viewed from different angles. Louise stood in the open doorway with nervously crossed arms and averted her eyes, looking this way and that down the hall, embarrassed by our attentions to her work, however she'd invited them. Appleton nodded at each new figure he came to, in some strange and wordless agreement with what he saw. Brand made guttural noises deep in his throat, hiccuping laughs of unwilled and cynical appreciation. Denise—were her eyes moist?—reached her gloved hand to the upraised palm of a figure whose other hand was at the base of its throat. Was it waving assistance as it choked or offering a salutation from the heart? Denise drew back her fingers and asked Louise, "May I touch?"

"No, but go ahead," said Louise without looking.

With tears dropping from her eyes—they spotted her mask like the first raindrops on a sidewalk before a storm—Denise pressed her palm to the sculpture's.

Brand had passed from art appreciation to simple prying. He poked his head around the corner of the bedroom, flipped the light switch, and called, "What the hell's going on in here?"

Over his shoulder, in the now-illuminated room, I saw that there was no bed or any other furniture. Heaped in the middle of the bare floor was a tangle of twisted, discarded metal, most of it hospital detritus: wheelchair frames, aluminum crutches, IV stands, hulls of X-ray machines, shelves, casters, faucets, traction chains, bed trapezes, curtain rings, clothes hangers, knee braces, neck braces, all kind of screws and pins and rivets and dowels, scalpels and scissors and saws.

"Raw material," said Louise. She finally came all the way into the apartment and shut the door behind her. "Scrap steel, medically sourced—what I made the piece from."

I turned from the bedroom to the sculpture nearest me: a figure on one knee with its hands clasped before it, either thrown down in torment and praying for relief or kneeling in an access of prayer and gratitude. Its face, I saw—a metal crescent with loosely swirled dollops of welded steel for its startled eyes and mouth—must once have been a plate in some machine. The face was welded to a spine that I now clearly perceived as one bent upright of a crutch, with pliable curtain-rod ribs soldered on, and arms and legs fashioned from wheelchair frame parts wrought into sinew. Having the source of the illusion revealed didn't dispel its power, though; Louise's people stood, walked, fell, and cried all around us in the room. She had infused these scraps of garbage and wire with the ineffable breath of life.

She offered to explain and led us into the apartment's kitchen, which she'd converted into a studio. More piled scrap steel lay on the counters and in every corner; at the back wall of the room, near the chairless table, stood a metal tank with a knob and pressure gauges, connected by a hose to a torch. Louise's helmet and gloves and boots and heavy corduroy overalls were arranged as neatly on the table as a soldier's kit. Also laid out were an array of saws and grinders, buffers and brushes. The table sat under the kitchen window, to which an exhaust duct for ventilation was fixed.

Louise opened a battered old laptop that faced the table from the counter.

"I usually livestream my process," she said. "You can collect a bit of extra money that way. I don't know if it's art appreciators or guys just happy they've found something new online to jerk off to, but it's fine with me as long as I get the money."

"I've watched you, my dear," Denise said. "I've fallen asleep with my anxieties silenced by the roar of your torch." She picked up the torch carefully, with both hands, as if it were a gun she was anxious not to fire by accident.

"But I'm not under my own name," Louise said. "I thought committees that awarded grants and prize juries and gallery curators would look askance on porn-adjacent online solicitation."

"Yes," said Denise, still studying the torch's burnished nozzle, "but you link from your professional website to a personal social media account, now defunct, that nevertheless alludes to pseudonymous avatars of your adolescence. From there it was a short step to your video channel."

Appleton, Brand, and I swiveled our heads to stare at Denise. She lowered the torch and waved one hand in an elegant gesture that made the clinging plastic glove seem like a queen's jersey gage.

"What? You boys don't think a poor old woman can work the goddamned Internet? You just go *click, click, click*—there's nothing to it at all."

"The Hyacinth Girl," Louise said in a small mortified voice beneath her black mask. I thought I saw Brand's eyes snap to attention.

"Don't be embarrassed, dear—every bookish child should have a T. S. Eliot phase. Mine never ended." She put one hand to heart and held the other out into the air. *"I have seen them riding seaward on the waves—"*

Louise in the meantime pulled up a video of herself at work and showed us: her helmeted head centered in a shower of sizzling sparks as she beaded the face onto one of her creations.

"You should appreciate metal sculpting, Justin," she said to Appleton. "It's just like cinema: writing with light."

Brand opened the kitchen's refrigerator and stuck his head inside. "Poetic, very," he said, "but I thought you were going to explain your work." He disgustedly slammed the door shut: the refrigerator wasn't plugged in and Louise had stocked it only with more scrap metal. "If I may be so crass, Louise," he said, "who's paying for all this? Or are you a trust funder, Louise?"

"I've worked for everything I have, Mr. Brand." She turned back to the laptop and called up another video. "This was a commission. I was chosen based on my past work. Just listen and you'll understand." She pressed play and set the video to widescreen.

A woman smiled patiently out at us. She wore what looked like a doctor's white coat refashioned into a cream robe; it swayed from side to side as she walked, in time to the long plaits of silvering black hair that reached almost the middle of her back. She folded her hands before her chest and walked on soundless espadrilles down a green-screen hospital corridor.

"Modern medicine," she said in an unplaceable accent, "is engineering. Marvelous engineering—the most marvelous the world has known—but engineering all the same. If a tumor or a bullet or a clot of blood or an arterial plaque are blocking the vital passages of your body, then you need an expert engineer to remove it and restore function. But just as the soul of a city is in its citizens and in their culture more than merely in its structures—more than in roads and bridges, however culture may depend on them—so health is more than engineering. How were you living your life such that your body developed a tumor or found itself in the path of a bullet? Physicians should aim not merely to restore bare function, but to create the conditions of flourishing: a body and mind both vigorous and at peace, flesh impregnable to whatever may threaten its vitality. Why, then, do our so-called healthcare facilities seem to go out of their way to make the conditions of flourishing impossible? Who, being ill, would wish to come to a cold structure resembling a prison or a barracks, to be processed by the blank machine of the modern hospital, to be prodded and palpated by the dry fingers of engineers whose professional pride consists of brisk frigidity? With iatrogenesis America's third leading cause of mortality, is it any coincidence that our hospitals have a reputation among ordinary people—and not only because of the viruses notoriously rampant within them —as the proverbial roach motel: a place where you may only check in, never out?"

As she spoke, a mournful electronic cello keened almost beneath awareness, while a low rumbling drum machine intimated distant thunder. Images coalesced and dissolved behind her: the exteriors of brutalist hospitals like Soviet housing blocks, slovenly emergency rooms crowded with the retching and the maimed, viral cells multiplying in exponential neon arcs across a microscope slide, the wasted faces of bed-bound patients staring with empty eyes into their canceled futures, a white-coated man with an affectless gaze coldly ausculting a child whose visage crumpled to a teary rictus of fear.

Then back to the woman walking in her billows of gown and hair: "It doesn't have to be this way," she said. The sun had come out in her corridor—a brief halo of golden light flared around her silver mane—and she gave us a tour through a different world. Now the hospital rooms were painted in warm carnation or cool fern; potted plants dangled down from the ceiling, their fronds gently stirred by a humidifier's white respirations. The very beds boasted scrollwork and statuary; moisture beaded on the windows as in a greenhouse.

"I am Dr. Hae Won Jeong," she said, "and I am proposing a new hospital for a new vision of health: for the health of the whole person."

Louise said, "You don't need the medical or architectural details," and dragged the video forward past a montage of nurse's uniforms in silver and gold and sapphire, convalescents taking the air in Japanese-garden courtyards, and surgical theaters like baroque altars under skylight vaults. "Some of this is a provocation—Hae Won knows it will never get done. But they wanted the full range of her vision when they brought her here from the West Coast—and she wasn't cheap, by the way—so this is it. Here's the part that explains *Scraps of Steel*."

"It's a mistake," said Dr. Jeong, "to think that a healthy mind or body is merely at rest. This view leads hospital administrators to settle for bland watercolors on the walls, when we should rouse the patient to health by dint of exercise, and not only for the neuromuscular and skeletal systems but for the whole person—the mind, the spirit. To that end I propose to hire the most compelling local artists in all media to create works that stir life to active contemplation. True art does not just please, like a pretty picture or a pretty flower. It embodies the contradictions everyone must live with and so brings everyone's attention to a point of intensity that rouses the spirit and inspires the will."

Louise scrolled again through images of her colleagues' or rivals' works—abstract paintings that tranquilly resembled the body's red-walled canals and capillaries; an installation that played clips from the whole life cycle, from baby's first cry to elder's death rattle on a loop—until she reached herself at work in her studio, her helmeted head steadfast with concentration in a fusillade of sparks.

Dr. Jeong said, "And then there is Louise Portofino, herself the daughter of a physician. Her brilliant sculpture cycle *Scraps of Steel* is welded from medical waste metals into a gallery of humanity pictured at our most vulnerable or most triumphant, our sickest or healthiest, depending on the viewer or the moment. Our plan is to distribute her sculptures throughout the hospital, placed as appropriate. When I asked Louise the significance of the title, she told me, *That's what's inside us, among the incredibly fragile tissues and fluids: scraps of steel that are indestructible and give us the strength to fight and rise up.*"

Louise paused the video. Denise tapped her gloved palm with two gloved fingers and said, "Bravissima." Appleton, obscurely, quoted the Gospel of Thomas: "*Split a stick of wood*

—I am there." Brand clicked in his throat some more, grunts of sarcastic appreciation.

"So the money is coming from where?" he asked.

"Hae Won is still raising the money for the projected new hospital. She spends all her time flattering and scolding and cajoling philanthropists and politicians. And with the quarantine, who knows? Maybe some people will decide it proved we didn't take health seriously enough, or maybe they'll figure we haven't focused enough on the basics to pursue aesthetics. That's the way one prospective donor dismissed her ideas: *aesthetics*, as if that were nothing and not everything. If you're asking who funded my piece, I got two grants—one straight from the state and one from a medical humanities foundation. Otherwise, I teach at the Art Institute every fall semester and sometimes get a bit of help from my mother. To rent two places in this dump, for example. I bet if the landlord knew I was welding in the basement, he'd throw me out. Luckily, he never shows up. I could show you my bank account if it would satisfy your curiosity."

Out of all her candid disclosures, Brand chose a digression to answer: "Aesthetics," he said, "are far worse than nothing."

He had been distractedly examining various items in her studio, but now he leaned his elbows on her table and narrowed his eyes at her across its expanse. She returned his provocative stare in kind. What were their mouths doing under their masks? Smiling or sneering?

"We should be going, my dear," said Denise into the hot silence. We were all sweating and breathless in our masks and gloves. "I'm exhausted all of a sudden." She went to Appleton and leaned on his arm; they led us a slow walk back among the stricken or exultant gallery of souls Louise had made from scraps and steel. In the hallway, Denise patted Appleton's forearm and said, musing almost to herself, "Justin does so much for me now. To think I hardly knew him before this quarantine. And now—my groceries, my cleaning."

Appleton stared embarrassed at the wall and said, "It's not that much."

Now Denise playfully rapped his knuckle. "Don't hide your light under a bushel. And you young people"—she turned to face Louise, Brand, and me—"don't neglect to have children, unless you want to rely in your miserable old age on finding a surprise helper." She bowed to us all, thanked Louise for the invitation and for the marvelous artistic spectacle, and walked with halting step and her head on Appleton's shoulder down to the hallway's skewed vanishing point.

Louise, Brand, and I looked from one to the other, our heads turning in amused confusion—were we all supposed to have children *together*?—until Louise said, "Would you like to come in for a drink?"

5. The Sword of the Apprentice

Louise tore the gloves from her hands. She pried the mask from behind her ears and dropped it to the floor; she kicked off her heels and sank exhausted, bare-faced, bare-handed, and barefoot, into the heavy black and dusty cushion of a wicker lounge chair in the middle of the small, sparse living room. She had the only studio apartment in the building, to make space for the laundry and boiler rooms also on the basement floor. I remained standing. Brand went to the refrigerator.

"The precautions were for Denise," she said. "I'm in that place I go to when I finish a big project and can't imagine how I'll ever have another idea or enough energy to execute one if I did have it—when I honestly don't care if I live or die. I couldn't care less if I catch it now. And you boys can take care of yourselves, I assume."

She stretched her weary legs and crossed her left over her right; I noticed that she was missing the middle toe of her left foot. Because it was in fact her middle toe, her foot retained a mutilated symmetry—a stricken shapeliness, but a shapeliness nonetheless. She'd followed my eyes to her injury and laughed behind her hand, a little embarrassed.

"Careless," she explained. "An accident with an angle grinder—should have paid more attention, should have kept my grip, should have worn sturdier shoes."

"Have to suffer or it's not art," Brand muttered behind his mask with his head in the refrigerator. "Van Gogh's ear, Kafka's lung, Portofino's toe…"

"But toes I can live without. I could lose all 10 and still work sitting down. Fingers would be a bigger problem, and I came close once or twice."

She held out her right hand to me and lowered every digit but the ringless ring finger: its tip was flat and textured like a guttered candle stub.

"But the nightmare would be to lose an eye—or both. It happens. I've read stories. Christ, I've seen pictures. One spark can sear the cornea forever if you're not careful, and I'm *not* careful. I would go on if I were blind, but it wouldn't be the same. And who knows? Maybe it would come out different—come out better—if I didn't have sight to rely on. What would a sculpture look like created by touch alone? Like nothing anyone had ever seen, I bet. But then I wouldn't get to see it. No, I'd like to keep my eyes, my eyes more than anything. When you consider what we can and can't afford to lose, why don't we have two toes and 10 eyes? Otherwise it makes sense, how the body is arranged: in ascending order of importance."

"An idealist!" Brand spat.

"A pragmatist," she replied with a shrug. "I'd rather see than walk."

He had come out of the refrigerator swirling by its neck a magnum of sangria garishly decorated in a fruit-and-flower motif. "Can I drink some of your sorority sister grape juice?"

"Did I claim to be a connoisseur in wines? In pandemic times, I need help falling asleep, and I like sweet drinks."

Brand raised his mask so that it covered his nose and eyes; he drank greedily from the bottle, goateed in fruity runnels. Louise watched with her own lips parted. Was she lost in admiration for his audacity? Should I have politely excused myself, left them to their Beatrice-and-Benedicking and whatever might follow from it? A mattress with mussed sheets waited at the back of the room.

Instead I asked him, in the silence marred by his sucking and gulping at the bottleneck, what he thought of Louise's sculptures since he hadn't actually told us. He stained his white sleeve in pale purple blossoms when he wiped his dribbling chin. He tore the mask from his face and threw it to the floor. I kept mine on.

"What do I think? What do I think, neighbor? I think it's kitsch, neighbor. To be perfectly honest. My apologies to the St. Sebastian House's artist-in-residence. Well-done, well-worked kitsch, but kitsch all the same. Fit for the corridors of international philanthropy. The triumph of the human spirit. The kind of thing the CIA liked to pay for back in the old days."

He arched an eyebrow at me and smiled with one side of his mouth; I looked away.

Louise rolled not only her eyes but her whole head on the back of her chair.

"Feel free to elaborate—but I bet kitsch is just a fancy way of saying, I'm afraid I'll fly to pieces if I have a human emotion."

He pointed a latex-tipped finger at her with the hand that gripped the bottleneck: "You know, that terrible habit middle-class women have of wanting to talk about emotions when someone raises a question of truth—*how does everyone feeeeel?* —it's condescending, it's insulting, it's actually entirely enraging."

Louise leaned forward and seized the bottle at its base with both hands out of his sticky gloved grip. "Mommy issues, I bet," she ventured before taking a drink. Not removing her eyes from Brand—wanting to see, I guessed, how he might meet her provocation—she passed me the bottle absently. I took it and walked it back to the refrigerator. I never drank: better, I thought, always to stay alert.

"Spare me your feminist psychobabble, Louise. Believe me, I've heard it all before, and from women with better credentials than yours."

"I'm not a feminist, just perceptive."

"Not a feminist? A woman of your education and generation? Maybe you're more interesting than I gave you credit for."

"The only *ist* I answer to is *artist*. You can't let the other *ist*s get in the way of that one, or you won't be able to see reality to recreate it any more. And if you divide the world—your subject matter, your audience, your very own soul—into exclusive categories, then you will lose before you even start. You will give up the power to show everything to everyone. Which is the only power I'm interested in."

Brand mockingly goggled his eyes and dropped his jaw.

"My God, Louise. I actually prefer feminism to what you just said, Louise. You believe this nonsense? This bourgeois ideology, this schoolgirl cant? A critic less kind than myself might say these insipid attitudes are reflected in your so-called art."

"*Au contraire. De gustibus.* My works are the songs of every man."

"Emerson? Whitman?"

"Bette Midler."

Their heinous flirtation receded into noise. I noticed a silver gleam on top of the refrigerator and reached up with both hands. Something spiky pricked my fingertips, made little holes in the glove for pathogens to invade. I took down a dusty sculpture of a figure, about a foot tall, fashioned from ordinary wire and nailed through its feet to a black-painted wood block. Aside from the thick strands of metal braided together to make the spine, the wire that formed the body was thin and wrenched and tangled roughly into the shapes of ribs or thighs. The sharp ends of raggedly-cut steel filaments jutted at all points like an evolved animal defense. The sculpture looked like a hasty, crude, vivid, gestural pencil sketch incarnated in three dimensions. The figure leaned acutely ahead, with one knee bent forward and one leg stretched back. Both arms extended out in a V, one raised above its head, the other lowered below its waist. It looked tensed in conflict with an invisible enemy. A small tarnished metal key was clutch-pinned to the thin wire of one leg. I carried it carefully over to where Brand and Louise continued their contest.

Louise said, "My great-grandfather came as an immigrant and sold fruits and vegetables from a mule-drawn cart on city streets that hadn't been paved yet. My grandfather worked in the steel mills. My mother went to school and became a doctor. It took three generations and three different types of hard labor to produce me and my work, and I work hard, probably harder than you've ever worked in your life. You're insinuating that I should feel ashamed to take money from my parents, to take money from foundations and from people who want to make the world a better place? Well, I don't. Not only do I not feel ashamed, but I'm proud of what my family and I have done."

Brand threw up his arms in outrage and began to pace all around her wicker chair. He began to rave and spit, both hands sawing the air, his heavy Oxfords stomping the bare floorboards. She bowed her head patiently under her dark curling hair, under his circling rebuke.

"But your work is worse than meaningless. It's an insult to your peasant great-grandparents and your proletarian grandparents. It's a set of decorations that make the world seem or feel better than it is while the same grinding poverty and exploitation goes on unchanged. Art is the most terrible, the most contemptible, the most disgusting thing in the world. I want to vomit when I think of it. Art makes all the other forms of oppression possible, bearable, comprehensible. It's the ultimate alibi, which is why the rich—when they aren't just using it to launder money—are still willing to pay for it. Imagine some mother without money or insurance holding her feverish baby in a hospital waiting room, choked with anxiety about the one thing your mother's rich friend didn't mention in her slick video—how treatment would be paid for. And imagine her confronted in that waiting room with one of your ambiguous gimmick figures—*Oh, is it laughing or crying? It's just like life, isn't it? We never do know how we feel, do we? How profound!* What will that mother feel when she looks at that? On top of the alienation she feels from a society that will punish her with a lifetime's debt if she asks its well-paid professionals to care just once for her sick baby, she will feel alienation from an ugly, incomprehensible object, one more trophy of the rich and one more sentry guarding the gate of health and peace against the likes of her. This is what you've done, Louise Portofino, you toeless twit!"

He stopped his march around the chair directly in front of her and took up her foot with the missing toe in both his hands as if to drag her to the floorboards. She brought her other foot up and struck her heel to the middle of his forehead; she knocked him down flat on his back. She stood up and bent over him and pressed her foot to the middle of his chest.

To his spate of accusations, she replied in a hoarse near-whisper: "My great-grandparents and grandparents didn't want a revolution or believe one was possible if they did want one. They didn't think the world could be made right, because it was *this* world and not the perfect world they hoped to go to when they died. They believed in charity—that it was the job of people who had more to give to people who had less—but they would have thought of a fixation on suffering as morbid and perverse. *Count your blessings*, they always said, *count your blessings*. They wanted money, and they wanted their children and grandchildren to have more of it than they did. They came here to be free, and having the time and space to make 15 steel sculptures of people who fight and suffer and laugh just like my great-grandparents and grandparents did is the highest form of freedom. Maybe they wouldn't understand my work, but my work is what they wanted, whether they knew it or not. My art is what they came here to accomplish."

She still stood over him, looking down into his eyes; he looked up from the floor into hers. I wasn't sure if this was still a flirtation or had progressed to incipient homicide, but I had begun to tire of them both, of their dueling self-righteous, self-impressed certitudes. I had thought for a moment to protect her, but she spent her days hauling steel, while he looked as if he might collapse from malnutrition at any moment; she had the physical advantage over him, as she proved by pinning him to the floor. If I'd been perfectly sure they wouldn't go for the kitchen knives and gouge at each other's eyes, I would have left them to their questionable passions. As it was, I stood with the wire sculpture in my hands like an embarrassed bridesmaid who'd accidentally caught the bouquet.

When she lifted her foot from his chest, he rose coughing, and she had to help him get steady on his feet. Then they saw me with the sculpture.

"Oh, that," Louise said. "*Struggle*. I made it in high school art class—my first metal sculpture. Every day for a month my hands bled from the wire-ends stabbing into my skin. My teacher said I'd need a tetanus shot. But I won a Silver Key at the Scholastic Art Awards. Second place—not bad for a state-wide competition, everybody said. Everybody but my mother, who said, *Why not gold?*"

She let go of Brand once he caught his rattling breath and came to take *Struggle* out of my hands. She rotated the figure to see it from a different angle and smiled the sad smile of someone staring at a photo of her much younger self: moved at the innocence, incensed at the stupidity, appalled at the suffering to come.

"This one maybe *is* kitsch," Louise said to herself. "But it was a start."

She carried it back to the refrigerator and re-mounted it, like a household god, on the dusty top.

"While we're touring your tchotchkes," Brand called from the front of the room, "what the hell is this?"

He pointed his ever-accusing finger up at some kind of crude two-foot-long blade mounted on the wall next to the door—a single bar of metal with its last few inches left for a grip but the rest of its length filed to a cutting edge. The blade had turned black and thick and rust-crusted with time.

"That," Louise said, "is how my great-grandfather came to America." She walked over to the wall and carefully took the primitive sword down by its rough handle. "It was back in the old country, and he wasn't much older than you"—gripping it in both hands, she pointed the blade in my direction. "He was apprenticed to a blacksmith, so by day he was sweating at the forge and anvil as he hammered horseshoes and wagon axles and candelabras and spades and gates into shape. But on the weekends, he would go see his sweetheart."

"His *sweetheart*?" Brand asked with coughing derision.

She swung the blade in his direction. "His lover, his paramour, his inamorata. His girlfriend, for Christ's sake. She lived on the other side of a graveyard—you could overlook it from her bedroom window—and he would cut through

78

among the fallen headstones and weeping angels to get to her parent's house in the night, after they'd gone to sleep. But a couple of the other young men in the neighborhood were jealous that he had won the affections of such a charming girl. So one Friday night when they knew my great-grandfather would sneak through the dark cemetery, they hid in different places—behind a crypt, on the other side of a monument, down in the unkempt grass—and when they heard him running in the weeds and stumbling at gravestones, they set on him and surrounded him and started pushing him around their circle from one pair of hands to another, until he fell on his knees and scrambled out between their legs. He ran back the way he came, still choked by his first moment of fear, before he recognized the young men as local bullies who'd tormented him all his life, that the dead had come out of the ground to punish him for skulking over consecrated earth on his way to make love to a girl not his wife. In the sunshine and sobriety of the morning, though, he realized what had happened and decided he wouldn't let it happen again. The next Friday, he waited until the blacksmith quit for the day and stayed behind. He took a piece of scrap iron and filed the edge down razor sharp at the grinder. He wrapped it in paper like a fish and set out again for his lover's house. Again he took the shortest path, through the high grass and sunken stones and toppled statuary. He went more slowly this time, though, hardly thinking of his Laura or Isabella or Beatrice— he only had eyes for the boys who'd set upon him the week before. And that time, when the first of those resentful brawlers leapt out from behind the wing of a marble angel, my great-grandfather was ready. He had his coarse sword out of its paper wrapper before his attacker was on him, and he sliced it through the air"—Louise spun the sword in a whistling semicircle; Brand and I both took a step back—"and the brawling boy stopped in mid-stride. He looked down just in time to see in the moonlight his intestines uncoiling into a slick heap on a grave marker, and then he toppled down on them himself. When his friends saw what had happened— when they saw my great-grandfather standing over the body with the sword still held at the limit of the arc he had drawn through his attacker's midsection—scattered in all directions. My great-grandfather re-wrapped his sword and ran back home. And when he confessed to his father what he had done, his father sent him to America on the next ship out, a step ahead of law or of vendetta, whichever came first."

"Well, Louise, I have to tell you, Louise, that sounds like a load of bullshit. You can put it in your fourth-generation reconnect-with-your-roots memoir or your immigrant-experience magical-realist first novel when you get sick of inhaling acetylene and steel dust, you can regale Oprah with it, but nobody will believe that story. Then again, who am I to talk? My people started burning witches the minute they washed up in Salem."

"It might have been embellished in the retelling down through the years," Louise allowed as she tenderly replaced the patina'd sword of her accidental paladin of an ancestor in its honored place on the wall.

Brand remembered I was in the room.

"And how did you find that story? Not too upsetting? What were the kids saying for a while there?—*triggering*? Not too evocative of, well, you know what?"

Louise, intrigued in spite of herself, also turned and studied my face with narrowed eyes.

They had taken off their masks, but mine still covered my nose and mouth; my breathing came thick, wet, hot, a constant rushing in my ears. But all they could see were my eyes, and I fixed them into an ocular posture of casual disinterestedness.

"Not at all," was all I told him. Who was he to know, to throw it in my face, as if the way my mother died were my shameful secret, and not the shameful secret of those responsible? Yes, I took their money—as Brand must have known—but did that make me their confederates in her death? "Not at all," I repeated.

Louise must have seen some mote in my eye, because she showed me a smile of compassion I tried not to take as patronizing—or, as it were, matronizing—and then she said, "Well, boys, it's getting late. I'd say we've violated quarantine long enough."

Brand hadn't lowered his gaze from my face. "Not my neighbor," he said. "He stayed safe. Mask and gloves. Hardly got near us. Didn't give himself away."

"A model citizen," Louise returned. Was she making fun of him or me? She opened the door and stood beside us, anti-inviting our departure. I had done the same to Brand the night

I met him, but now I found myself grouped with him among the night nuisances. She yawned theatrically and ran a hand through her tangle of black curls. She idly scratched the back of her calf with her four-toed foot. Finally—as Brand and I stood immobile, watching her—she put her hands on her hips and tossed her vast hair at the aperture.

We passed obediently through the door. As he went by, Brand said, "How old are you, Louise?"

"33," she said.

"Your Jesus year."

"There was a time I thought I wouldn't make it to 30. Then I wanted more than anything to live—to travel, to read, to fall in love, to make my sculptures. And now I just want to live a day past Jesus."

This struck Brand as funny. His laugh decayed into a wheeze, which spasmed into a sputtering cough. He doubled over, clutching his wasted chest in his thin arms. Louise shut the door without well-wishes or ceremony; she must have sobered out of her early indifference, borne of giddiness from having finished her vast project, to the risk of catching the novel virus. I stood aside and waited for Brand's fit to pass. I turned and took a last look through the door as she closed it. I had a glimpse of what hung on the wall opposite her grandfather's hastily-forged sword: *Christ of the Abyss.*

6. The Shield of Achilles

Shelter in place, social distance, personal protective equipment, continuity of government, exponential curve, quantitative easing, hiring freeze, comorbidity, serology, dyspnea, anosmia, hydroxychloroquine, azithromycin, cytokine storm.

The quarantine was extended, the viral load increased, the novel language deepened, my heart rate elevated. The death toll climbed on both logarithmic and linear scales. Given projections of resource scarcity, experts were deciding by brute actuarial calculus who was fit to live, who was not worth saving.

I still wasn't taking my father's calls. They were a formality anyway. He knew where I was and that I was still alive. He had friends with access to my phone and laptop data, friends who could fly drones past my window, friends who could put me in the cross-hairs of satellites. He could be watching me at any moment.

The unemployment rate went up. The university first informed me that "unprecedented budgetary constraints" forced them to terminate my teaching appointment for the fall, though I was welcome to remain enrolled in the graduate program at in-state tuition rates. Then they informed me a few days later that my spring class would be taken over by another instructor in light of the adverse public reaction to a video I'd posted for my students during the transition to remote learning. I had uploaded Brand's monologue from the night he'd invited himself into my apartment and told me his life story. If *that* wasn't an Introduction to Modern Philosophy, what was? None of my students complained, but one found it so hilarious she shared it on Twitter, where it proceeded to go viral, as we used to say before the novel virus rendered epidemiological metaphors forever tasteless. Probably most people laughed at Brand's speech, and more than a handful agreed with his critique of everything; but then it ended up first on a right-wing website—"Shocking video of socialist indoctrination! Funded by *your* tax dollars and targeted at *your* kids!"—and then on a few liberal ones that objected to Brand's description of the poor as a "different species" and to his evident hatred of women. Everyone agreed I should be relieved of my position.

Without even the pretense of teaching the class—without my idle perusal of its discussion board, my feints at reading the passages from Descartes or Hegel I'd assigned—I lacked anything to structure the days. A few days passed without my hearing from my neighbors in the St. Sebastian House after *Scraps of Steel.*

One night I slept deeply enough to dream, a rarity in those days. I dreamed that Louise Portofino and I were walking through a hydroponic garden in Dr. Hae Won Jeong's utopic hospital. We wore masks but smiled at each other anyway. We gathered the ingredients for a salad we intended to eat together; we picked lettuces blooming from the mouths of bed-bound patients. The sun came through her coils and curls of dark hair. Somewhere water dripped in an echoing stone basin. Then a cry wrenched me out of the dream: like Orpheus I reached for her receding figure as a dark tunnel sucked me back up to life. Outside my window, down below in the alley, a dog whined and moaned and snapped and snarled, impatient for Brand's proposed canine *reconquista* of the earth.

Police began to enforce the quarantine. They dragged the insufficiently vigilant—the over-eager shopper, the hapless partygoer—into crowded and soiled cells, to slow the spread of the novel virus. The corporate monopolies began to collate their collected data to detect public noncompliance. Drones drifted overhead, shone spotlights here and there, and blared friendly reminders from the state.

The rent was past due. I'd forgotten, and then I remembered. If we were coordinating a refusal, no one told me, so I dropped my check to the never-seen and nameless landlord (St. Sebastian Property Management) in the entryway's outgoing mailbox. I met Appleton there. He smoked a cigarette held between trembling fingers; Brando as

Col. Kurtz glared red-faced and dead-eyed from his T-shirt. He said Denise had given it to him to calm his nerves, though he'd had to light it on the red-hot coil of the ancient electrical stove-tops we all had in our apartments. Smoking was said to be a comorbidity of the novel virus—it was probably the type of activity one's phone, laptop, and smart TV would soon be reporting to the public health authorities—but I didn't suggest that to him. He was finally forced to shut the Royal Cinema for good, he told me, and he could pay April's rent, but not May's. To cheer him, I suggested we ask Louise if she had any more masks and gloves; if so, we could convene in his apartment for a screening.

"What movie?" he asked.

I reminded him of his analogy between cinema and worship: "You're the priest."

Louise's mask and glove hoard proved enough for another gathering, so five nights after the first of the month we spread out as far from one another as we could in Appleton's dim living room to face his vast television. He had dragged his mattress to the kitchen so we'd have more space. Denise looked thinner and more infirm than she had the week before

—even her eyes had clouded over. She sat half propped on a pile of musty blankets Appleton had heaped into a faulty seat. Her gloved hands trembled in her lap. She'd put one over the other to stop the tremor until the one on top, the one meant to bring order, itself buckled and quaked. Then she'd switch and repeat the cycle. Louise watched. She turned to me to see if I was watching. Brand hadn't yet arrived.

"What are we viewing tonight, dear?" Denise asked Appleton, her voice thick behind her mask. "I appreciate your earlier comic selections, but you don't have to treat us like frightened kittens. People speak of the need for diversions and light entertainment in pandemic times, but I find I crave almost the opposite: a mirror to my confusion, an affirmation of my fear, a story adequate to my gaping disbelief that reality is what it is, has come to this. Acknowledgement that someone else has recognized, has confronted, has survived, has been able to articulate that abyss we're hanging over by our fingernails. So lay it on us, dear Justin, whatever you have, we can take it—whatever nightmare from the depths of modernity you've been holding back from us."

She fell further back into her unstable makeshift throne of blankets, flushed and breathless. Appleton, who had nodded throughout her speech in agreement, opened his mouth to say something. He caught his breath and looked over our heads.

Brand stood in the doorway, without mask or gloves. We all turned from the television to him. He wore his belted tan pants and black Oxfords on bare feet, but no shirt. His jutting ribs striped his wasted torso in shadows. He held a laptop in one hand and traced arabesques on the touchpad with the other. Focused on the screen, he said distractedly, "There's been a change in the program, Denise. I'll be curating tonight's show, Denise. You haven't heard of the director, but if this doesn't mirror your confusion and confirm your fear, I can't imagine what will."

He walked up to Appleton and directed him to broadcast his laptop screen on the television.

"And why the hell should he do that?" Louise asked. "What gives you the right?" She went from sitting to crouching, as if she might spring on Brand.

Appleton folded his arms and refused to accept the laptop.

"In here I only play my own choices, man. You'll have to figure it out for yourself."

"Perhaps I should re-introduce myself," Brand said. "I'm the landlord here. I own the St. Sebastian House. And if Justin does me this favor, I may overlook the likelihood of his falling behind on the rent. If not, not."

Appleton shook his head bitterly; from the evidence of his eyes, he wore a sneer of disgust beneath his mask. But he took the laptop.

"So what *are* we watching, dear?" Denise called weakly from the blankets in which she was half-immured. She was starting to sound delirious. "Home movies from your splendid childhood? Nights on the Vineyard? Hyannis Port in July?"

"Not *my* childhood," he said, smiling out of one side of his mouth. He'd handed the laptop to Appleton to work out the Bluetooth connection with the TV and walked over to me. He leaned down, and whispered. His breath, unmasked, hissed and scalded down my ear.

"You tell it," I said to him. "You'll enjoy it more."

"Where even to begin?" he asked himself. Just then Appleton projected the laptop screen onto the television, and I saw at the size of the wall the first frame of the video my father drank three shots of whiskey to steel himself to show me at our kitchen table on my 18th birthday. I'd watched it, drunk the shot he'd offered me, and thrown up in the sink. I let myself fall flat on my back, onto Appleton's rough-hewn dusty floorboards. Brand, narrating the story of my life, paced around me, as if I were an exhibit in a surgical theater. Denise had fallen silent in her nest. Appleton eyed the television, excited in spite of himself for any novel cinema. Louise remained in her coiled crouch, staring up at Brand with glistening eyes above her mask—a look I interpreted as outrage and wonderment.

"To understand our mutual friend here," Brand began, "you have to understand his parents. They were a classic romance of mismatched lovers. *Mésalliance,* as they say in France. She was in defense, he was in intelligence. You could mistake the old man for a professor. Much of what he did—I should say *does*—is indistinguishable from scholarship. Our friend here must have encountered him throughout his childhood only as a closed study door. Behind that barred door, this scholar drafted memos and reports for use here, there, and everywhere. He explained how to manipulate Catholic practices and indigenous traditions to convince the *favela*-dwellers of Bolivia and Venezuela that socialism was not their friend. He brainstormed the conversion of electoral democracy and open markets into a language he thought the benighted nomads of Afghanistan might possibly understand. And wasn't Confucius more compatible with the Jeffersonian pragmatism than with the Marxian ideology, wondered this gentle and bookish man, and couldn't this somehow be brought home to the Politburo? Did he confine his speculations to those far-flung places where we Americans enjoy or endure so many national interests? I don't think he did. My admittedly crude Internet sleuthing turned up at least circumstantial evidence of the old man's professorial hand in crafting a seductive rhetoric for agents provocateurs to wield against popular movements left and right—against any movement that might call into question whether or not the national interest was really the citizens' interest. It's rumored on certain disreputable message boards that he even dabbled in literature—counted a New York editor or two among his friends and was occasionally asked if this or that novel came a little too close to disclosing a state secret or two, even if only in spirit, never mind the letter.

"So it must have surprised his colleagues when this learned gentleman took up with a lady on the military side. I'm not an expert, but I think the suave intellectuals and humanists of intelligence tend to regard their more bellicose rivals in the area of national defense as knuckle-draggers. Opera vs. country, tennis vs. Nascar—you get the drift. But our friend's mother was no jingo flag waver. A science-minded schoolgirl from the start, she had begun her career as a technical writer compiling dry reports on such-and-such of a weapons system and its capacity to destroy the enemy or the defense budget, whichever came first. She was still working for the government when she met her future husband—probably at some tedious Washington black-tie affair—but by the time they were married, by the time they had a son, by the time they moved to the suburbs, she had transitioned to the private sector. It was there that her superiors at a cutting-edge defense contractor called Achilles Shield—no apostrophe, I note for the purists among you—discovered her hidden talent. She had always been torn, you see, even as a schoolgirl, between science and art. The wonders of the sea that must have made her want to be a marine biologist at 12—to discover the hidden mechanisms of pulsing flesh even in ocean trenches— also inspired a passion for description. She wrote poetry well into adulthood, and even published some in little magazines. I printed a few out, but I left them down in my apartment. Remind me later, and I'll read you *Love in the Abyss*, the finest poem about a giant squid copulating with a female human I believe I've ever encountered. *Suckermarks: ankle, knee, and hip; / She'd lain in the swirl of his 10 boneless arms*. That's verbatim. But she became a technical writer for bomb-makers, not a marine biologist and not a full-time poet, if there is any such creature on land or sea. With their eye for talent, though, the upper ranks of Achilles Shield spied the light under her bushel and turned her back from technical writing to the lyrical kind. These masters of war had to sell their death machines, didn't they, and selling is more than facts and figures, isn't it? It's about vision and emotion, empathy and connection. Art is the essence of selling. So they asked her, our friend here's mother, to put a human face on their avant-munitions and futurist bioweapons. Justin, please play the video in the YouTube tab."

I watched the golden dusk from the screen play over the pitted ceiling of Appleton's apartment. I felt no need to see the commercial again, the commercial that ran for most of my adolescence on all the 24-hour news channels and during the Sunday morning political talk shows: I had it memorized. The advertisement both repulsed and fascinated me when I was 15 and 16, in the years just before my mother's death. I'd begun by then to examine all the assumptions that had underwritten my childhood, as anyone does in adolescence, and quickly became consumed with shame and anger as the meaning of my parents' work gradually coalesced in my consciousness. I burned my eyes out long into the night staring under the covers at my laptop, reading essays and watching lectures by everyone, credible or not, left or right, who might drag my parents to the bar of justice for the global crimes they enabled. I checked out the only Noam Chomsky book in our suburban public library and kept it wedged under my mattress when I wasn't reading it, the way my father must have done with his teenaged *Playboy*s and *Penthouse*s. Yet wasn't it my father's job to find out what the enemy was hiding? Wasn't it my mother's job to mete out the fatal consequences for such deception and betrayal?

She only mentioned casually one night, when I happened to pass through the living room, that she had written the commercial then playing on the TV. I paused and watched its 30 saccharine seconds.

Morning in America, fanfare for the common man, amber fields of gazing grain, a plow silhouetted against the sun, children in superhero capes and princess dresses waving little flags at a Fourth of July parade, a bent but unbroken veteran making what might have been his final salute, apple pie *à la mode* melting on a diner's chrome bar, shirtless boys on a tire swing out over the water, an off-road truck almost lost in the haze of the dust it raised, a young bride dancing barefoot with her stoical father as one teardrop glimmered at the corner of his eye. It might have been an ad for anything—cars, jeans, ice cream, home equity loans, diabetes medication. But the narrator intoned, "Defend what matters most," over the swelling music and the final shot: a yellow-walled suburban house filmed from below as time-lapse clouds raced in the sky and a flag fluttered wildly from the awning of its porch. It was our house—the house I grew up in, the house in which I was then watching that very commercial. Then the Achilles Shield logo—a silver medallion with an involuted and abstract design suggesting a city map or a printed circuit—materialized slowly on a black screen.

I don't remember what I said to my mother when it was over, when the TV pundits started shouting at each other again. I remember that she'd turned her head to await my reaction, and her face was involuntarily creased with anxiety. Did I use the adolescent's license of total sarcasm to make some smart-ass remark? No, I'm sure I praised her noncommittally. I'd have been happier had she told me about her poems, which I hadn't known to exist until Brand told us all in Appleton's apartment. He knew more about my mother than I did.

Yet her commercial held some fascination over me, because once I found it online I couldn't stop watching it. I couldn't respond to its imagery with anything but amused contempt. Too young to have been affected by 9/11, I came of age in its squalid aftermath. I had read too much to look at kitsch Americana without seeing its bloody underside—the depleted uranium munitions poisoning the Iraqi earth forever, the sweatshops and maquiladoras where our consumer goods were made by people who might as well have been enslaved outright, our own prisons full of a desperate underclass we could shelter or accommodate in no other way compatible with capitalism and so regarded as disposable. But some truth in the images—or at least some sincerity of feeling behind their "artificial wilderness," maybe some maternal plenitude I still wanted to believe in—seized me, and I watched the commercial again and again. *Defend what matters most.* One time I was watching it when my mother came unexpectedly into my bedroom to deliver some laundry, and I slammed the laptop shut so hard it nearly cracked the screen.

After Appleton played it for the residents of the St. Sebastian House, Louise said, "So what? The lady needed to make some money. There will always be defense contractors—isn't it better that they have beautiful commercials rather than ugly ones?"

"Spoken like the mercenary you are," Brand said distractedly—he'd taken the laptop back and was pulling up the first video, the one my father showed me on my 18th birthday.

"You don't even have the balls to use the word you want to use," Louise said.

Convinced now of his cowardice, she relaxed out of her crouch and sat with her legs crossed. I turned onto my side and drew up my knees, my back to the room, and stared at the dusty wainscot, at the gray fur crossing the unswept floorboards.

"If I call you a whore, will you mend your ways?" I heard Brand say. "Anyway, all artists are filthy whores."

She ignored his provocations and asked, "Why are you doing this? Telling us all this—which is none of our business?"

"But it *is* our business, Louise. It's the nation's business, Louise. Here is a man living alongside us whose whole life is a state secret. He pays me rent—where does the money come from? From an ugliness in the world that few will admit exists at all. From a horror that underpins our lives as surely as the foundation holds this building up."

"His mother died in an accident," Denise said from behind her mask, beneath her heap of blankets, as if calling out in a dream.

"That's what you told me when you came to see me, Denise, so proud of your digital investigations. And that *is* what it said in the newspaper, Denise. But you're too smart to believe everything you read in the newspaper, and so am I. For my part, I thought the story was a bit, well, incomplete. The woman died on the premises of a major defense contractor, and all we hear is that it was an accident? I wanted to know more—I *needed* to know more. I began my researches. I was open to a mundane explanation. Maybe she fell down the stairs. It could happen to anyone. But she didn't, in fact. And the way she died had leaked out sufficiently to become an online legend. Maybe on purpose; maybe the higher-ups at Achilles Shield thought it burnished their fearsome reputation, even at the cost of making them look careless. How careful do we want them to be when they're destroying threats to national security. So in my researches, I found the mainstream media useless, but the kids on the chan boards were always obliquely referencing some mythical video taken the day she died, a video that would periodically surface and then be removed, surface and then be removed, on various sites. A video of her very death. When they found it, the kids used it as a dare and a challenge. *Can you watch without throwing up? Or are you a pukecuck, a vomfag?* You know how such people talk. I knew better than to create an account and earnestly ask them for it.

"Instead, I went hunting for this proverbially unwatchable video of an unexampled death that would overwhelm the stomach of the most seasoned viewers of porn and gore. I wasn't exactly a stranger to the dark web anyway. I had contacts among hackers and pranksters and gunrunners. I had funneled money to the legal defense funds of enterprising digital pirates, and I had covertly helped to fund both sides in various street altercations between rival extremist groups. But I searched for the video even amid the forbidden pornography and black-market weapons for a few days with no luck. I paid somebody to hack a university database to download her mollusk erotica poems from whatever obscure literary journal they'd been published in 30 years ago—that was my great find, but no iconically hideous video.

"Then the Internet suddenly gave me just what I wanted without my having to put in any effort, like a chest of gold washing up on shore. Somebody simply uploaded the footage to PornHub one day, and there it stayed for about a week, under the charmless label *Bitch's Bisection*. I downloaded it before the moderators could take it down, and I'm happy to tell you I have a stronger stomach than the fearsome Internet trolls of America because I watched it five times without so much as acid reflux. It's quite fascinating, in fact. We might see it as the opposite of your *Scraps of Steel*, Louise. Maybe this is my counter-exhibition, maybe they should play this in the hospital lobby. What humanity's really made from: scraps of meat."

The last thing I heard Brand say was, "Justin, please press play." I put my hands over my ears. I didn't need to see or hear it again. Every frame had etched itself in acid across the walls of my skull.

The footage was supposed to be used in a triumphal documentary, or a new commercial, or a presentation to solicit more government or foundation money. The camera operator stood behind my mother and followed her into the building.

She would serve as guide and narrator. Many suburban parents commuted downtown for their jobs, but my mother went the other way, deeper into the state's interior. For a while the only sound on the video was the dry rustle of grasses and passing cars and the clack on the pavement of my mother's smart pink pumps.

The industrial park comprising the offices and laboratories of Achilles Shield sat in a declivity below the highway, a bowl of land fringed with high, wild, and desiccated grasses, beneath the strip malls and gas stations and motels of the exurbs. It looked like the public high school I attended: a long, flat, beige box, nondescript as a warehouse.

In the laboratory lobby, sterile as a waiting room, Dr. Geoffrey Cabot greeted my mother warmly, with a casual handshake that ended with him clasping her right hand intimately in both of his. Achilles Shield's lead scientist, Dr. Cabot, was later indicted and then jailed, not for his negligence leading to my mother's death that day, but for his sexual trespass upon several underaged women during his tenure at the firm. A girl had escaped from a filthy motel near the turnpike and reported him to local police, who, being provincial, arrested him on the strength of the forensic evidence left in the stained and rented room before any higher authorities could intervene to save their savant. Cabot pled in the media and in court that he had unfortunately allowed his otherwise winningly Faustian drive to innovate for science's own sweet sake to eclipse his ability to interpret socio-emotional cues or to behave according to evolving ethical norms. His prosecutors in turn reminded the jury that his alleged crimes, which included beatings and strangulations as well as forced penetration, and of girls young enough to be his granddaughters, were proscribed not by newfangled feminist dogmas but by the most elementary forms of Christian morality and English common law—if not, to be sure, by the scientific will to truth. Speculation online that his victims were trafficked to him by magnanimous investors as a perquisite of his running the most advanced private defense research lab in America, or the world, was never substantiated and its advocates were dismissed as lunatics damaging the norms of democratic discourse with their recklessly expressed hallucinations.

That day, Dr. Cabot was blessedly ignorant of his coming fall; he smiled and rocked and bounced, his black and silver wave of hair shivering slightly with his motion, excited as a schoolboy who'd made his mother a clay vase in art class. He skipped in his dress shoes, almost sliding on the floors into a vast high-walled laboratory whose tables—bristling with microscopes, plastics, lasers, torches, tongs, vices, hammers, and more—were ranged around a circular dais in the middle of the room. Dr. Cabot led my mother to this strange raised clearing. The air in that magic circle seemed to hum. The lab workers looked up from their work in pride and concern. Dr. Cabot showed off his team's newest development to my mother—as surrogate for an audience of investors and government officials—and the camera crew behind her.

The latest development, he explained at my mother's encouragement, was a barrier made of materials invisible both to the eye and to radar and satellite surveillance. These materials—the chemistry was too complicated to explain, he explained—could be thinned to as little as three millimeters in width and yet stand with absolute steel or granite solidity as high as 50 feet. He invited us to envision jeeps, tanks, convoys, missiles, and even low-flying aircraft speeding across the deserts of Mesopotamia or the mountain passes of Central Asia only to crash, crumple, and burst against what would appear to be nothing but the middle of the air. He grinned to think of it, to picture those confused and bearded terrorists shattered against the sky, with his teeth so white and square that they too, I thought, must have been engineered with lasers and polymers like everything else in that vast laboratory.

He swept his white-coated arm up the high walls, up toward the 20-foot ceiling, to indicate triumphantly this newest development, this last word in defense technology: nothing at all. The camera panned upward. In that nothing above his and my mother's heads, he said, was a wall only a few millimeters thick that no human or electronic eye could see and no conventional shell or warhead penetrate, a wall that would soon come on the market and protect us against all enemies, foreign and domestic.

Dr. Cabot stood back and encouraged my mother to come forward and touch this invisible pane. She stepped onto the dais and cautiously walked forward with one hand extended.

"It's just above you," he told her. "Lift your arm." But she must not have lifted it enough, because he stepped behind her, took her hand, and raised it high over her head. He put his other hand on the small of her back.

When my father first showed me the video at our kitchen table, our table from which my mother had been absent three years, I had squinted, determined to see this invisible wall just as I was learning from my books and websites to see the invisible ideology that permeated the world my parents made. I could see nothing but a slight shimmer, like heat haze, where her fingertips met the air above her—perhaps some premonitory tiling in the digital footage. Only the groaning cry of one of the scientists in the back of the lab told me something had gone wrong. Then I heard a sound like ice creaking as it thaws and cracks. Dr. Cabot deftly released my mother's body and took three quick steps back.

My mother turned to face the camera with a questioning look just after the scientist's cry, the creaking snap, and Cabot's retreat. A second after that strange noise, that icy splintering, she opened her mouth to say something to the camera, to her audience, to me. Instead of words, two streams of blood poured out of each corner of her parted lips and stained the front of her professional white blouse like two roses fast-blooming in time-lapse. The front and rear halves of her body made a slow wet puckered sound like a suction cup coming unstuck as they each slid from the invisible pane that divided them. Her front half, light as a child, trailing sinew and gristle and gouts of blood, dropped into arms that Dr. Cabot extended by reflex, while her back half struck the tiles like a raw rib-rack that had slipped from a slaughter hook.

The air above the dais cobwebbed with a million tiny cracks and the crinkling yaw of a thawing pond. A sudden rain of glittering glass strafed the camera, a sharp squall that tore the lab workers' clothes and skins as hail riddles the leaves. The camera panned to the scientists: they stood dazed and torn and raddled in the fine glass dust, amid rills of blood beginning to run between the tiles of the floor.

Louise gently took my hands from my ears. "It's over," she said. I sat up. The room glowed blue with the TV's blank screen, receiving no signal. It was like the bottom of the ocean. The light glimmered on the tears that wet Denise's cheeks. Brand stared silently out the window; a drone passed, level with his head, spotlighting the street below for quarantine violators. I could hear Appleton retching in the bathroom.

"It's *not* over," Brand said. "It will never be over. It's always happening—it's the deep truth of what's always happening."

Louise still held my wrists.

After he showed me the video on the day I turned 18, my father explained how we would be paid for life to keep our silence about the "national security incident" that was my mother's untimely demise. He pulled a small package from a box marked with Achilles Shield's logo from his bedroom closet and handed it to me—my birthday present. I opened it to find my mother's smart pink pumps, in four pieces, each neatly cleft in two through the arch.

7. The Ministry of Night

A week passed—or two weeks—or a day. Who could tell? Sirens, drones. The quarantine was extended. We would be confined in 15-day increments for the rest of our lives. Dante somehow left this element of delusive but irresistible hope out of his *Inferno*.

At two in the morning on a Tuesday or a Saturday I found a conspiracy theory online almost as good as the ones I'd first discovered in my rebellious adolescence. Getting a taste for conspiracy theories is not like discovering the rare pleasures of chocolate mousse or duck confit, a feast you want again just as it is and only on very special occasions. Conspiracy theories are like heroin or pornography: you want the next one now, and it has to be more complicated and expansive than the last, more daring in its breach of credibility even as it is more undeniable in its explanatory power. This new theory said that world pandemics have always been correlated with the introduction or intensification of radio wave communications, from the so-called Spanish influenza's coinciding with the spread of radio per se in 1918 to the novel virus's dissemination along pathways already broken by 5G technology. The theorists who agreed on this historical narrative—and I didn't check their facts: why ruin a good story?—disagreed about what it meant. Did the technologies themselves cause illness, or were the viruses a cover for some remote assault on the human body engineered through the air by the powers that be? I appreciated the theory for its hint that zoonosis was not, as expert opinion held, the cause of this novel virus, like the also-ran viruses before it—that it did not leap to human hosts from bats or swine, like Gadarene demons in reverse, but was rather a case of *technosis*. We caught the illness from our machines, just as we caught insomnia and paranoia and distraction and rage and hate and lust from them. Like only the choicest conspiracy theories, this one, irrespective of its relation to fact, held a poetic truth.

Poetic truths were an inflated currency in pandemic times. Everyone tried to support everyone else "in this difficult moment"—"in these unprecedented circumstances"—"in these challenging days"—by posting poignant historical facts, wise and stoic apothegms, or inspiring tales of difficulty overcome. The kind of copy, I reflected, that my mother could write. And who was I to complain? What had Denise said when I first met her? *Call on whatever god will get you through the night.*

That day's rousing story, which I'd found after burning my eyes to their sockets on 5G conspiracies, only lengthened the night with rage and frustration. A 392-year-old shark, said news reports, was found in the Atlantic Ocean; it had been slowly plowing the gelid depths of the northern sea since before Newton formulated the laws of motion or Milton dictated *Paradise Lost*. What was the point of this story? Why was it meant to comfort me? *Life goes on*? *Humble yourself before the wonders of nature*? I stared at the photo of the shark—this gray, scarred, pitted zeppelin of meat and teeth that had been drifting above the undersea canyons without a thought in its bullet head but to feed and mate for five or six human lifetimes—and thought how much more valuable it would be to have had Newton or Milton for so long, to have had a creature with a capacity for thoughts adequate to the complexity of the universe, to have had a mind able to appreciate, comprehend, and, most importantly, recreate the world in which it found itself, rather than this cancerous mass of blank ingestion. Next Brand would be telling me this ancient shark had, in humanity's *quarantena* absence, swum up the Grand Canal of Venice and devoured St. Mark's Basilica—which was all wretched humanity deserved for never having become just.

It was two in the morning on a Wednesday or four in the morning on a Sunday when Louise knocked on my door— three almost imperceptibly soft taps. When I opened it, I found her holding her index finger to her masked lips in the dimness of the hallway. She carried her boots in her gloved hands and cautiously tiptoed into my apartment in her socks; I followed her all the way to the kitchen.

She took my naked hand in both her covered ones and whispered huskily in her mask, "I'm going to need you to trust me."

She explained that two weeks ago she hadn't been able to sleep and had found a crumpled half-empty packet of cigarettes in the back of a drawer. In her anxiety and insomnia, she resumed her previously overcome habit—"A stupid choice in a pulmonary pandemic," she conceded—but decided at least not to indulge in her own apartment. She went outside and walked around to the alleyway to light up. That's when she noticed Brand come out of the St. Sebastian House in his button-down shirt and tan pants and stomping Oxfords. He'd looked over both shoulders and then, in spite of the quarantine, disappeared down the deserted street. She could hardly follow him in her pajamas, so she watched around the same time on the subsequent nights. Exactly a week after she'd first spied him as he went, she saw him set out again.

"That was last week. If he does it again," she said, "it'll be in five minutes. I want to see where he's going—who knows what viral load he's picking up and coming back here with. But I don't want to go alone."

She carefully fixed a mask to my face as we waited silently behind my front door to hear Brand's own door open and close. I drew on the pair of gloves she'd brought me. We counted 10 seconds after we heard Brand's bolt shoot back into the mortice; then we went out in time to see the back of his head receding down the steps leading to the entryway.

It was hard to follow him without notice, considering that barely anyone walked or drove those streets in the dead middle of the night in pandemic times. On a few occasions, when he seemed like he might look behind him at the mysterious sound of footfalls, we had to dodge behind walls or garbage cans. Once, a police patrol car slowly rolled by, and Brand hid in one alley while Louise and I hid in another. Later, a drone whirred and buzzed overhead, its white spotlight browsing the sidewalk; if it detected us, it held its peace, as if it too had tired of the quarantine's anxious discipline. Despite these obstacles and the circuity of the path—Brand favored dark, mazy back streets to avoid the attention of the law—we soon understood that we were witnessing his ministry.

Over the course of 30 or so blocks, he visited three properties, presumably his own. All resembled the St. Sebastian House: low, dirty buildings, dressed in crumbled brick, that dated to the middle 20th century or earlier. All three possessed an air of having once been a reform school, rectory, bordello, or lazar-house. They squatted resentfully in the shadows cast by the bright-paneled plastic-toy structures rising all over the city, though some of these were now abandoned mid-construction in one of the quarantine's only welcome effects: a rectification of taste. At each of his squalid domains, Brand produced a key ring from his pocket and jangled it with abandon in the dark to feel his way to the right key. Only once was he stopped by a cop, while Louise and I crouched behind reeking aluminum garbage cans, but he bashfully charmed his way to freedom as only those born to the estate he loathed could do.

We couldn't follow him inside his properties unobserved, but we prowled the peripheries to catch glimpses of him through the windows. These partial views, though they were like film frames spliced together at random, did eventually cohere into a narrative.

In the first building, we saw him tenderly wet the lips of an old man in a basement apartment who could not rise from his bed, who could only mumble his half-insensible gratitude. We watched him patiently take a wash cloth and bathe the wasted limbs—a skeleton hung with gray crepe—of a dying woman as she moaned in her bed. In a bathroom with walls the color of diseased urine, he helped a half-paralyzed woman onto a toilet and sat with her and held her hand with politely averted eyes and pleasant chit-chat as she did her business. He matched the playful boxing stance of a corpulent old man in suspenders as they shared a beer and watched a half hour of an old movie on a TV still comprised of glass and vacuum tubes. He bathed a woman who must have been a century old, a heap of bones loosely swathed in mottled skin, which he treated as an immortal soul; he dipped water over her head like an old-time preacher midwifing the born again.

In the second building, he rocked a colicky baby in his arms like one born to be a mother; later, he changed a diaper with deft fingers and an instinct for diverting play. Through another window we watched him try his luck at tiddlywinks with a girl of six or eight while her mother paced around her bed in the apartment's only other room, begging someone or other on the phone to give her another chance or send her another check. While the little girl's back was turned, we could see Brand slide three 100-dollar bills under the game board. A young couple took what must have been the first opportunity they'd had in all the weeks of the quarantine to make love while Brand in another room read their toddler to sleep. The little girl fought drowsiness, her head sinking slowly and then jerking up rapidly. She giggled helplessly as he did the voices of the farm animals in the book—*squawk, moo, neigh*—and then she subsided into a smiling rest. He finished reading the book to himself even when her head nestled in the crook of his arm. He bathed a child who couldn't have been more than a month old; he sprinkled water on the baby's forehead as if they were at a marble font and not in a bathroom with walls and floors the putrid green of a polluted lake.

In the final building, he pressed cash into the palm of a girl with pink tinder hair, a body stunted at the age of 12, a face weathered to about 80. He read from the Big Book with a man in a T-shirt with a ripped collar and wild hair and a four-days' beard, and together they emptied the vodka and whiskey bottles into the sink. He held a young woman by both hands, and held her gaze too, as he earnestly reassured her of something that eventually dried her eyes; even from our spies' perch, we could see the furrowed scars down her wrists.

Also in the final building, we spied a 40-something woman offer him rent in another currency. He refused at first, but she said she did not want to be an object of his pity or charity. She wavered between flirtation and desperation; she couldn't hold on to all the forms of her dignity, but she wouldn't want it to be said of her that she did not work for what she had. With tears in her eyes, she shook her hair, gray coming in at the roots—no bright dye in pandemic times. She kneaded his forearm with trembling fingers. He agreed to her arrangement; he collected her rent with ambivalent groans. He gently pressed her face against the wall. Her window was open—they were right beneath us in her basement apartment —so we heard him say, "Government guidelines," as he slowly drew her hair between his fingers, and we heard him grunt, more to himself than to her, "Comme un chien," and we heard her cry out as her pink acrylic fingernails raked the flaking paint.

The last building was near the river. The new bright-walled, glass-balconied developments encircling it seemed as if they would soon crowd it into the water. Brand almost eluded us as he hopped down a stone embankment like a boy and walked the river path back toward the St. Sebastian House. Every rough sleeper tossing on the concrete greeted him by name as he distributed cash to them from his pants pockets.

The river churned southward. Swollen with northern snowmelt, the water exhaled damp green rot into the spring night; the peaks of its frothing waves raised shards of moonlight. We lost our breath following Brand's frantic strides. Eventually, though the night held a chill, he tore his shirt off, scattering buttons like small coins along the path, and balled it up and hurled it into the water. It bloomed; it floated briefly like an albino algae; then gravity sucked it furling downstream.

By the time we reached the entryway of the St. Sebastian House, Brand had wrapped his arms around his emaciated frame—he clasped the craggy tip of each shoulder in the opposite hand—but he shivered anyway. From 30 paces behind him, we could hear his teeth rattle. Denise sat on the front steps smoking a cigarette. She looked less frail, more her old self, bobbing her harem slipper on the end of her stockinged foot. Brand clambered up the concrete stairs as if she weren't there, but she tugged his pantleg until he sat next to her, wracked and shuddering.

"You think I don't know what you're up to, Arthur Brand?"

She pointed her cigarette in accusation at his face; ash drifted in his lap. Louise and I had approached the building obliquely, and they hadn't seen us. We hid in the shadow of the steps, our backs to the cold concrete.

"I never hid it," he said through chattering teeth. "Most people just don't care to look. Anyway, what am I doing, Denise?"

"You'd never have done anything in particular if it weren't for the quarantine."

"No, I wouldn't have, Denise. And I'm still not doing anything."

"Well, precisely. You gallivant at all hours, ministering, I assume, to your less fortunate tenants. Oh yes, I may be an old lady, but I can find out all sorts of things. Public property records, for one. What the places look like for another. What some of your boarders whisper about you in the obscure depths of social media. Small newspaper items about your generosity. But are they, your wards, taking precautions in what everyone calls *this difficult time, this unprecedented time*— in other words, pandemic times? I was raised very long ago by less fortunate people myself, and my recollection is that they combine an inability to take or to afford the hypochondriacal precautions of the well-to-do with an instinctive mistrust of the threats and warnings of experts. But you—you should know better. You're putting them in danger, to say nothing of yourself."

"They say it's five days from symptoms to pneumonia, three days after that to death. Do you know what a relief, what a release that would be for some of the people I've seen? Death would be a blessing, a gift. The greatest mercy of all."

"It's not your choice to make."

"I include myself."

"And what about us? Why keep a fourth building? You have one for the elderly, one for young families, one for the addicted or the desperate or the criminal. But for whom is the St. Sebastian House?"

"For people who don't deserve my generosity."

"The house of privilege. Not for the nearly dead or the only just born or the self-destructive among the impoverished, but for those like you, those who could even, if they wanted to, afford something better. The slumming artists and intellectuals. You'd deliver death to us not as a release but as a curse."

"I include myself."

"But us?"

"The old professor, hypocritical middle-class leftist, who's given up on a world she never seriously wanted to change. The projectionist, worshipping an *ignis fatuus* he takes for real light. The young student, so morally indolent he allows himself to be bought by his mother's murderers. The sculptress, wasting her gift on steel alibis for new exploiters with smoother tongues."

"And you gathered us here deliberately?"

"I chose carefully among those who applied. I can find things out on the Internet too."

"You didn't find that video of your neighbor's unfortunate mother a week ago."

"I found it the week before he moved in, though the story of how I found it was true."

"And am I to believe you had nothing to do with what happened to Justin tonight?"

"Believe what you want, Denise."

"He used his one phone call on me. Nothing so beautiful has happened to me since I buried my lover. He said he'd heard the abandoned storefronts in the neighborhood were being looted and invaded by squatters, and that he considered it his obligation to check on, to secure, the theater. He said he was careful, he said he didn't turn on any lights that would be visible from outside. Yet they knocked down the door of the projection booth—they drove their truncheons all the way into that inner sanctum of the theater—and dragged Justin away. He said one smashed his skull with a club. He said another beat the projector to pieces as if subduing a maniac, a threat to the populace. You know he lived for that theater, Arthur."

"Toy worship. Idol worship. American childishness. I know you enjoyed his misplaced filial affections, Denise, but has it occurred to you, Denise, that he was in that, as in everything else, just a blubbering overgrown infant?"

"So you called your friends, the police. To tell them someone was violating quarantine in the Royal Cinema. Now he's in some squalid jail where the pandemic spreads like fire. You've as good as killed him."

"Why do you call them my friends?"

"What are the police but a rich man's friends?"

"There's the old Denise Green, author of *Beyond Pity and Peace: Prospects for 21st Century Revolution!* Oh yes, I read it— the day you sent in your rental application I went straight to the library! But Denise, help me understand one thing. Here you are, elderly, in the highest risk group—if one may comment on a lady's age—and here I am, having gone out and exposed myself to every viral agent in the city, shivering as if malarial, and you talk to me with not six inches between us, much less six feet, and no mask, no gloves."

"I don't fear death, Arthur. It's contemptible to fear death, in fact. But that is a decision you and I may make for ourselves. What I question is your making it for the others. Especially Louise, the one of us you hate the most, for reasons so obvious I won't belabor them. So I would ask you—I know it's all I can do, I know I don't have the strength any longer even to crush a flower—but I would ask you, from one disappointed idealist to another, to let them go before you murder them with the infection you're willfully releasing into the St. Sebastian House. Don't do it for them, but for the sake of your own soul."

He didn't say anything, and she didn't either. The only sound: his teeth clacking in his tremulous mouth. With what felt like infinite slowness and precaution, I crept high enough on my knees to lift my eyes over the stone steps. I saw Brand, in the dim light from the entryway and the dim light of the moon, raise Denise's long hand, obviously once elegant, now a fasces of bone strung with veins, and kiss it with practiced delicacy. The wet print of his lips glimmered above her knuckles. She tossed her cigarette butt into the street, stood with such difficulty that she had to use Brand's skeletal shirtless frame to steady herself, and limp back into the building. He soon followed.

When Louise and I thought enough time had passed to allow him to go back into his apartment, we entered the building too. But we had misjudged. He still stood uncertainly in the dim slanting hallway, between his door and mine, sweat now shining on his forehead, on his pale hairless chest. Hunched, his spinal column chondrichthyan beneath his shrunken skin in the jaundice-shaded overhead light, he stared at my door with feverish eyes, from out of his hollowing face, as if he didn't quite know what he was seeing. A bland truculent resentment twisted his lips, and he half-sneered, half-smiled, out of one corner of his mouth. He trembled, jostling the beetled rack of his ribs, and then reared his head back so far it would have paralleled the floor had the floor been true. He snapped his head forward with a viscous growl in his chest and spat a stream of cloudy sputum onto my doorknob.

8. The Canals of Venice

"The petite bourgeoisie, therefore, is the revolutionary's real class enemy. This class of small business owners, clerks, and middle managers—which increasingly includes the ranks of lumpen academia and the arts—will always desire to rise in the world by their own agency, and not as a class for-itself but as a non-collective aggregate of irreplaceably unique individuals. They will certainly not serve as junior members of an insurgency among the exploited whose labor they rely on for their inexpensive consumer goods. They will always frustrate the revolution, because they will always see themselves—an image of what they wish to be—in the grand

bourgeoisie. Despite their delusions of grandeur, however, they do not even exhibit the courage or savoir faire of proper capitalists. They want to own the means of production, but the best they can do is to manage businesses or, worse, to get office jobs. Yet despite all this, they justify themselves to themselves with a rhetoric not of ruthlessness but of sentimentality. They do it for family; they work for what they have; their success honors the sacrifice of their forebears; they show the lone honor and power of the individual, the difference a single solitary person can make. One would prefer the most heartless plutocrats, the undeceived blonde beasts, to these tiresome consumers of the nostrum and the bromide. For the revolutionary, then, it is the petit bourgeois who must go first, on the principle of removing the proximate enemy earliest. Their culture, at the very least, must be liquidated, because it blocks the path to the ultimate enemy. The revolutionary respects the ultimate enemy, but feels only contempt for this mawkish pasteboard army it has ranged around it. The problem, of course, is that writer of these words and the reader of them likely belongs to the class just slated for demolition."

"Jesus!" Louise said. "Denise wrote that?"

"She did—*Beyond Pity and Peace*, like Brand said. Published in 2005. *Denise Green, Professor of Political Science*. That's as much as I can read on the Amazon preview."

"Maybe it gets lighter as it goes on."

After the night of Brand's ministry, I had moved into Louise's apartment at her almost motherly insistence. She said Brand's intention toward me was plainly murderous, that we couldn't take chances after what he'd done to Appleton, and that in fact as soon as she had supervised the transfer of *Scraps of Steel* to its installation site she planned to move back in with her mother and offered me help getting back to my father's. I didn't tell her I had no plans to move back to the suburbs or that I had, ever since leaving at the age of 18, been unable to feel anything but a nausea toward my father for his acceptance of my mother's death and his willingness to be paid for his silence—in the name of "national security secrets," secrets so well kept they were all over the Internet to be enjoyed by cackling teenaged boys. What I felt for my father was what Brand felt for me, so how did I even have the right to refuse the death my neighbor offered me? On the other hand, if I could stand between Louise and his unwarranted malice toward her, then—though my years in academia had beaten such thoughts out of me, I thought it anyway—wouldn't that make me a better man than my father? I moved in with Louise.

She slept on the bed, I slept on the floor. At night, we kept a kitchen chair jammed against the doorknob. We drank sangria and ate rice and beans every night from her quarantine stash. We had lively, disturbing conversations, verging on argument. I said, for instance, that Brand was guilty of raping his tenant under our eyes on the night of his ministry. What real choice did she have but to comply with the man who decided if she had a roof to live under? Louise insisted, by contrast, that this was a dehumanizing argument in the guise of a humane one, that every choice was always constrained, that human ingenuity and endeavor—wresting any hint of beauty out of the mire of circumstances—ought to be acknowledged as heroism, not patronized as victimization. I later learned from what I could read of Denise's book that my opinion was the revolutionary one, hers sentimental petit-bourgeois reactionary individualism. Kitsch—that's what Brand had charged her with.

We rarely mentioned the novel virus, the pandemic, the quarantine. We stopped following the news. We might as well have been a mile under the ocean.

We quarreled about Denise. Louise said we needed to bring her down here with us where she would be safer. I said that she'd made her choice, that she as good as told Brand she had come here to die, and who were we to interfere with this wish? I suggested that, given Brand's slobbering over Denise's hand and spitting on my doorknob, he had likely seeded the St. Sebastian House with so many virions that none of us stood a chance of avoiding infection, and that Denise was better off where she was, at the top of the building, her viral load minimized. That was when we googled Denise and read some of her book—generally a quasi-Leninist defense of violence as tool of social emancipation—and Louise's charitable attitude waned.

One day Louise took a video call with Dr. Hae Won Jeong. The doctor, pleasant and unruffled, not a hair out of place, radiated the serenity she prescribed, despite the prevailing social chaos. She told Louise that while of course the grand new hospital project was on hold given the circumstances, she and her team would like to visit in two days and—safely—collect *Scraps of Steel* for display in and around the new field hospital being hastily erected in the city's major park to handle a projected surplus of the critically ill. Louise agreed, her own demeanor as pacific and smiling as her interlocutors. Then she shut her laptop and began a manic phase of work.

"I thought I had another month!" she said as she hurried into her work boots.

I joined her in the other apartment, her studio, as she put final touches, final beads and streaks and arabesques of liquid metal, onto her gallery. I watched the sparks wash against her face mask as the arc welder flared. I helped her carry her figures from the living room to the kitchen to have their forms corrected or completed. We were like physicians after all, transporting the prostrate from waiting room to clinic. She despaired of the treatment.

"You should see how it looks in my mind. This is nothing. It's too thin, it's fake, it's not real. It's just art, who cares about art? In my mind, they're not art, they're real. Sometimes it seems completely absurd to try to bring them into the world.

Like I should just lay down and keep dreaming of them. Let that be enough."

After bringing each sculpture to a point beyond which she could no longer add anything without destroying what she thought of as the fragile unity she had managed to achieve, she paused to lift her mask, to wipe her forehead, to drink water. Finally she asked me to knead the tension out of her shoulders. She lay across her studio table, and I gently pressed my fingertips into her bunched, knotted muscles; she ordered me to squeeze as hard as I could, no matter how much I thought it might hurt. My fingers ached; Louise moaned. She finished *Scraps of Steel* in one day.

"I can die now, I guess," she said. "At 33—my Jesus year."

The next morning the symptoms began. We were both stricken at once. I woke on the floor with a mass of damp dirt packed in my chest. I sat up and tried to cough it out, but my cough only seemed to scrape against the weight of it and abrade the back of my throat. Louise sat at her tiny kitchen table wrapped in her blanket—she wore it like a hood over her mass of hair—and shuddered so much she shook the table. I imagined the look we shared was like one passed between soldiers watching an unstoppable advance raising the dust in their direction.

Louise didn't have a thermometer or any fever reducers or any healthy food. She remembered an old Italian remedy: she poured the rest of her wine in a pot and boiled it. We took turns scalding our noses and throats in the vinegary vinous steam. We felt too sick to eat. Our fevers went up as the sun went down; I couldn't stop my teeth from knocking against each other like thrown dice.

Louise invited me to come from the floor into her bed. I told her—as best I could with my juddering chilled jaw—the theory that the sick in close proximity could make one another sicker by increasing their viral load. She said we didn't have anywhere else to go.

Febrile hallucinations, half-dreams, embarrassing and obvious: Louise naked but for her work boots and welder's mask standing in a shower of sparks as she soldered the two halves of my mother back together again. The novel virus permits us no secrets.

We slept for an hour and woke choking; we fell asleep so hot I thought our eyes would melt; we woke in soaked sheets.

The fever went in and out like the tides, moved like the tides by the moon, or so my parents told me when I was a child. Hand-me-down ignorance, comforting myth, scientific fact? Who could say? Once I woke—it was dark, three in the morning—and we were holding hands.

Later, she stood up from the bed and attempted to walk to the bathroom, but a combination of breathlessness and feet tangled in sheets sank her to her knees. I climbed across the bed and stood dizzily, as if I had to carry both myself and the heavy thing that had invaded me, the pulsating mass in my chest, that always closed my breath, now a block, now a slurry, its liquidus and solidus obscurely determined by the hour. Though all my joints felt torn at the ligaments, I gathered her up and, both choking, one body with four clumsy feet and two backs, we entered the bathroom. With one hand, she took down her pajama pants, and I lowered her to the seat of the toilet. Her flesh now fired from the inside, she pulled her T-shirt over her head. From burning, bleary eyes, she saw my burning, bleary eyes fall on the swirled scar below one of her dark nipples, the lightning jag of plowed flesh across her belly, the pale keloids on her thighs and kneecaps.

"I've never had an easy time with my body," she said.

I fell to the edge of the bathtub and held her hand while she peed—what must have been, I knew from experience, an uncannily hot stream, as if our insides were on the boil. She put her head between her knees; her curls sprang down and touched the tiles. With her nine bare toes she gripped the floor, barely clinging to the world.

"My mother is a doctor. She wasn't exactly *my* doctor—I don't think that's allowed—but her colleagues and connections listened to her, and she always thought, or from her point of view she always *knew*, that there was something wrong with me. She never looked at me once in all my life with simple interest or affection. Her eyes were always narrowed, her mouth always set, because she was tense and searching, she was looking for the sign, the mark, the movement, the muscle contraction, the asymmetrical blemish, the dilated iris—whatever would would show my sickness. I was her only child. Once my dad left, I was her only anything, besides her practice. As a doctor, working with strangers, she was just what you'd want: calm and steady and polite, someone who knew when to save the moment with a joke or how to say in a way that wouldn't destroy you that it was too late to save anything. Seeing all the ways the human body can abolish itself makes a lot of doctors philosophical if not nihilistic, superior to fear or concern, blasé jokers or cold pragmatists, people who'll tell you to pop pills till they stop taking the pain away and then lay down and die. It didn't have that effect on my mother, though. What she saw—the tumors and lesions and obstructions and sepsis and ruptures —slowly over the years precipitated a poison of obsessive fear in her, fear that it would happen to me. She could see it just under my skin, crawling over every inch of my body. And as a child, I made her suspicions real, I acted out her fantasies. We would collaborate—she would tell me what illness she suspected I had that week, and I would collapse with the symptoms. If tests were inconclusive, she would call in favors. Did I have appendicitis? I had a night on the bathroom floor when I felt like some set of hands was wringing out my organs. The appendix came out. Every mole and blemish removed, along with slightest bulge or ripple under the skin.

By the time I was a teenager, though, I couldn't share the game anymore. I both felt that I would kill myself if I didn't get out from under her eyes and that I had so internalized her eyes that I knew for certain I had at most six months or a year to live. My rebellion wasn't drugs—she'd have noticed that—and it wasn't sex—I thought if a boy touched me he would immediately feel my death creeping along between the bone and the epidermis. I've never taken drugs beyond alcohol, and I didn't have sex until I was 25 years old. But I defended myself by rejecting the intellectual basis of her world. Starting in high school, I almost failed biology, I just barely got a C in chemistry. I declared that I didn't have the slightest interest in any science, though I'd been a star student, an award-winning student, until then, so much that my mother and I would plot my route through the Ivy League to medical school. But when I turned 14, I spent all my time learning to draw and paint. I said I would be an artist or nothing at all. When I won the Silver Key for *Struggle*, she saw I was serious. She wasn't a tyrant, wasn't a monster—just a very anxious woman. She sighed and said at least I was learning anatomy and agreed to pay when I got into art school. And I went to art school to draw. As an anatomist, I had grand delusions of reviving figurative art, of burying the nihilism of the avant-garde. But when, just to fill an elective credit, I wandered into a metal sculpture class, that was when I knew I had to become not an anatomist but a surgeon. And since then, since I started assembling bodies out of scraps, since I started restoring life to discarded things, I've felt like I might not die anytime soon. But it wasn't easy getting here. They took me apart and put me back together a few times. And you're never what you were before."

She lifted her head from between her knees and nervously watched my face for signs of a response to her disclosures. In either a genuine febrile delirium or a fever I used as a conscious license to behave deliriously, I leaned forward and kissed the scar on her breast. She bent her head and tented both our faces in the coils of her hair.

"I read an article once," she said later, in bed, between hacks and gasps. "It was written by some woman in her 30s repenting for her 20s. She warned young girls—everyone is always warning young girls—not to waste their precious time on brief affairs with flashy men who can't be relied on, no matter how good they are in bed. Not that her husband, she said, wasn't good in bed, not that they hadn't been jump-in-the-fountain madly in love when they first met. It was just that a year or two into their marriage she got some kind of debilitating illness or injury and was in such bad shape that she couldn't even cross the room. Her husband, she said, had to walk her to the toilet and sit with her while she did her business so she didn't fall off and crack her head open on the bathroom floor. She advised young girls to always ask themselves, on a dating site or a first date or a one-night stand, *Will this man will help me to the toilet? Will he still love me after he does?* It's supposed to happen after you jump in the fountain, though. I wonder, will we even want to have sex now that we've already seen each other as—as rotting meat?"

"There's a lot," I said spasmodically, "there's a lot that people wonder about," my chest heaving up to choke me, "that we won't have to wonder about."

She turned over and pummeled my back to jar loose the mucus. She hammered with both balled fists.

We lay facing away from each other to minimize viral load, but we shared a common pool of febrile sweat—Christs of the

Abyss, I dreamed, swimming hand in hand through the canals of Venice.

I half-slept and half-dreamed.

I dreamed—or did this happen?—that my father called and I finally answered. I dreamed that when I heard his voice, I cried out, "I want to live! All I want is to live!"

9. The Land of the Deed, Reprised

I dreamed I went to visit Appleton in jail; I dreamed I had smuggled in Louise's great-grandfather's filed sword so that Appleton could cut through the bars and escape. The scream of the edge against the metal bars in my dream became a scream in real life and brought me upright in the damp bed before I was awake. Gray light, predawn: Louise was gone.

I heard her screaming out in the hallway, screaming at Arthur Brand, screaming and then choking and then screaming again. Between breaths, I stumbled to the apartment door. I opened it a crack and watched them, breathless against the doorjamb, trying not to fall. He was shirtless again in his tan pants and Oxfords, his skin shrunken and puckered around his ribs and spine. He put his hand against Louise's mouth and drove her against the wall next to the door of her studio. In his other hand he jangled a key ring manically—he assaulted the quiet dawn with noise and discord.

"I don't have the right? I don't have the right? Listen to me, Louise—have you ever considered, Louise—that I've been a grant-writer for several non-profits in this city for 10 years, and that I consequently might be very well acquainted with Dr. Hae Won Jeong? That I might have sat at her left hand at one or two philanthropical banquets, charitable silent auctions, ribbon cuttings, spina bifida benefits, and the like? That I may have heard your name before you even submitted your application for two apartments in the St. Sebastian House? That I might have even given Dr. Jeong the tip for cheap housing and studio space that she passed on to you? That, knowing me for a landlord, she might even have asked me first? That Denise is not the only one to watch your livestreams late into the night? Have you ever considered,

Louise, that your life isn't wholly your own? That no one's is? That other people have every right to it?"

He took his hand away and let her fold, tussive, to the floor. Between breaths, the door into the apartment where Louise kept her studio slammed shut. Brand had gone inside. She scrabbled up the wall, she staggered to her feet, she fell against the door, and then she was in with him. Between breaths—what was happening in the infinitude of time between my breaths?—I followed them.

I passed through what Denise, the day I met her, had called Louise's gallery of souls: alongside all those people crying out in joy and pain, prostrate with grief and gratitude, ourselves in the abstract, everything and nothing, all that is and will be, standing there on earth because Louise Portofino's own hands put them there. Their faces flashed and vanished in the corners of my burning eyes. For a moment, falling and rising, stumbling and running, I was one of them.

Louise and Brand were in the kitchen. I watched them from the shadows of the doorway. The sky was still pale in the last moments of sunlessness, the room, lit by the small high window that opened onto the alley, gray and dim. They had the table between them; they stood tensed against it, each poised to spring across. Brand had the acetylene torch in his hand and showered the room in sparks. Sweat dripped from his starved frame and his shaggy, overgrown blond hair; his visible skeleton trembled with deep, echoing coughs. His blue eyes bulged as his face receded.

"Why are you doing this?"

"Oh, where do I begin? With the invention of agriculture? Double-entry bookkeeping? The landing of the *Arbella*—the founding of our little city on the hill? Begin with this, Louise Portofino: I was lying awake all last night. I'd just found out that one of my tenants in another building cut her wrists and died in a red bathtub because she didn't have a job and didn't see how she'd find another one, and she didn't have anyone—not parents, not children, not a lover—she could rely on, and it was either stretch it out over months killing herself with the pills she'd only just kicked or end it quickly in the tub before the rent came due again. And I was thinking, Louise, I was thinking, when I couldn't sleep—and to be honest, I may have a fever—I was thinking, how is it that down in the cellar of the St. Sebastian House there's a procession of metal statues—of objects, of toys, which is all they are, *toys*—that are more alive than a woman I touched, a woman whose pulse I felt under her skin, less than a week ago? Who is it that makes us live this way? Why do we tolerate one more second of it? I've been thinking since this started that it's not so bad—let the trees grow up through the buildings until the buildings fall, let coyotes run down the avenues. But now I'm thinking that people are dead, and toys are alive. Does that seem right to you? Does that seem right to you, Louise Portofino?"

She suddenly veered around the table and tried to grab the torch from his hand. Had she been well, she would have overpowered him, but since both were sick he seized the advantage. They each wheezed and gasped and coughed as they spun around the table with hands clasped on the torch. He fought her back to where she'd started and then shoved her against the table; he wedged his knee between her legs to pin her where she stood and raised the torch level with both their faces.

"If only we had 10 eyes," he said. He raised the nozzle of the torch level with both their irises.

Between breaths only three strides brought me across the room. What was the weight at the end of my arm? Between breaths, I must have taken—for protection—the apprentice's old sword from its shrine on the wall before I'd followed them into Louise's studio. I now found myself heaving it breathlessly above my head, gripped in both slick fists. *Defend what matters most.*

I let the metal file's weight drop whistling through the air. Its fall halted when it broke but could not cleave Brand's clavicle. The torch slipped from his suddenly nerveless hand. He spurted the side of Louise's face not with fire but with arterial blood; it rose from his half-severed neck in a bright arc that glittered like spray or sparks through the light of the now-risen sun. He collapsed backward onto the table. The century-old makeshift sword, forged in fear and defiance, still buried in his neck, scored the wood.

From her half-mask of gore, from her fever-burn eye sockets, Louise stared into my face with a dumbstruck mix of awe and terror. Then a column of smoke snaked between us: a stray spark had set the leg of Brand's pants on fire. The flame rippled blue and orange along the underside of the table, not six feet from the torch's gas tank. Louise shoved me back and shoved me back until I turned and ran, ran back through the gallery of souls. She stayed behind but called after me, each word expectorated from fogged and drowning lungs, "Save. Den. Ise. You. Have. To. Save. Den."

By the time I reached the stairwell, I could only advance on my hands and knees. I scarcely drew breath. Several times, I half-thought, "Better to lay down, best to die." But I remembered Louise, I remembered her command to save Denise. Happily, Denise, on her own hands and knees, met me at the top of the stairs. Like prowling dogs we eyed each other nose to nose in wariness and confusion.

"What's. Hap. Pen. Ing?" she stammered out, hacking. Her hair a silver tangle, she was hardly dressed; she had wrapped a bedsheet around herself and crawled feverishly down a flight of stairs when she heard the noise or smelled the smoke. She couldn't hold herself up any longer and collapsed just as I gained the landing. Her eyes rolled, out of her control. I was on the first floor: I just had to get us through the entryway and out, a distance of less than 30 feet. Louise's injunction—Louise's and another: *Defend what matters most*—sounded like the faint rushes of blood in my ears. I laced one of Denise's arms in mine and grappled her to my back; I rose, still on my knees, and secured her other arm. In one flare of my almost extinguished energy I stood, weighed down less by the thin, exhausted woman on my back than by the liquid stone, the concrete ocean, in my chest. Diaphanous, a swirl of smoke now spiraled up around us from the stairwell. Some infant instinct told Denise to circle me with her legs, to press her heels to my thighs, and then, thinking I would at any moment die, I ran.

My run must have taken a third of a minute, between breaths. I remember nothing of it, except Denise's hot wheezing whispers in my ear, her quavering jaw, her staccato regrets, held up by the hitch in her voice, in her chest.

"I thought. To change. The world. What a. Stupid. Thought I. Stopped danc. Ing I. Moved where. Uni. Versit. Ies told. Me to. Move I. Never. Had a. Life un. Til I. Met my. Lover. Who died. And now. What?"

Between breaths I found myself on the lawn. I lowered Denise to the wet morning grass. On her back she had a surge of breath and said all at once, "What's beyond peace and pity?"

Out of the smoke now rolling from the front door of the St. Sebastian House, Louise Portofino rose with the acetylene tank in her arms, clasped to her chest, below her face half-masked in blood. To meet her ran a man wrapped from head to foot in a thick green army surplus shawl and a mask that covered the half of his face not concealed by dark goggles. He took the tank from her gently, like a swaddled baby. She collapsed to the dew next to me and Denise, as we all fought for any breath we could catch from the vernal air.

The masked man leaned down to me and asked, "You said you wanted to live. Well, you're alive. How does it feel?"

Above the cachinnating crackle of the now-burning building came sirens from all directions. I was now awake, now asleep. I looked straight up into the bright spring sky and saw a drone buzzing high in the distance.

"What's beyond peace and pity?"

The flames had only begun to consume the first floor, so firefighters were able to douse it before it spread. Still, they drowned all of my and Louise's earthly possessions, and with the St. Sebastian House's structure compromised and its landlord dead, it was sure to be demolished. Only Louise's gallery of struggling souls, tempered by fire, survived in that abyss.

A truck dispatched to pick up the commissioned sculptures coincidentally arrived at the same time as the ambulances. I could hear my father, in that brisk but friendly manner he'd always adopted in restaurants or banks, waving away the EMTs.

He returned to where we lay gasping and again leaned down. He said to me in his half-masked voice, "I'm not letting them take you to a city hospital right now. You'll die on a stretcher in a goddamn hallway. I have a connection."

He rose and hailed the baffled drivers who had come to transport *Scraps of Steel*.

My father's connection turned out to be Dr. Hae Won Jeong. He explained later, "I've met her once or twice—an official dinner, an awards ceremony, a fundraising banquet, that sort of thing. A very thoughtful woman, with more ideas in a day than I've had in my life. We worked with her on one or two projects. You know, public health campaigns in the developing world."

I didn't ask who *we* were; I didn't have to.

The truck sent to collect *Scraps of Steel* instead transported Denise, Louise, and me to a field hospital in the park where Dr. Jeong demonstrated the effectiveness of her proposed medical reforms. By the time I woke up, a day later, *Scraps of Steel* had arrived. In the partitioned-square of the vast white-walled tent where Louise and I slept in beds six feet apart, a metal figure either agonized or exultant, lifting its arms in despair or gratitude, guarded our rest. On the screen that formed our room were delicately translucent watercolor blossoms.

Dr. Jeong had banned ventilators in her revised hospital. "The lungs are not a bellows to be inflated mechanically—we are not machines," she later told an admiring press corps with the mayor at her side. Two humidifiers sent arcs of billowing white spume over us like a benediction; we slept as if underwater. "It's the whole secret," the doctor explained. "It creates an inhospitable environment for disease. It's why our grandmothers held our heads over boiling pots when we were sick as children."

From somewhere up near the transparent tent roof bright with sun, Debussy played on mounted speakers. Spring air from open apertures at either end of the field hospital washed over us all.

Dr. Jeong didn't believe in withholding harsh truths from patients as if they were children, so one day she told me with her brisk compassion that Denise had died in the night.

Another day or the same day—all was one feverish day— two detectives in surgical masks drew chairs to my bedside and asked me a series of questions about the day of the fire. My father stood behind them with a *what-are-you-going-to-do?* look in his eyes and his arms folded impatiently: mock exasperation at pointless bureaucratic formalities. They never asked me directly what had happened to Arthur Brand; if they'd asked, I'd have told them. But both his death and the fire were ruled accidents.

A brief article describing Louise's heroism in saving the building and mine in carrying out Denise went viral, but, in our lucid hours, Louise and I agreed to turn the interviewers away. Dr. Hae Won Jeong, who thought all publicity good for her good cause, was happy to talk to them anyway. Louise and I knew we weren't heroes.

When the quarantine lifted, the wreck of the St. Sebastian House was knocked to pieces. A pricey apartment building with lime-green and berry-pink walls, like a toy beach house, rose in its place. The same thing happened to Brand's other properties. Where his more desperate tenants went, I don't know. He would have known.

Dr. Jeong's regimen—art, music, air, light, water, and a cocktail of antiviral but all-natural medicines that would in therapeutic combination come to bear her name—rid us of the novel virus in a little over a week.

At 10 days, Louise and I shuffled in masks and slippers around the field hospital, weaving among the personae she'd crafted in steel, to bring food or water or an attentive ear to those who suffered more than we did.

"I can't say I never lose patients," Dr. Jeong told the media. "No doctor can say that. But in my hospital even those who can't make it back go out in peace."

At 12 days, we were discharged. As a physician, Louise's mother was quarantining from all but her patients, so she understandably did not visit us in Dr. Jeong's field hospital, and we agreed that Louise would go home—to the house in the suburbs where I was raised—with me and my father. My father warmly shook Dr. Jeong's hand and thanked her almost tearfully for saving my life; he'd grown more maudlin since my mother's death. She put both her hands around his and told him it was her pleasure.

My father drove us out of the city. The quarantine had begun to lift by then, but the streets still appeared deserted. The occasional passerby went masked, and the quality of the mask became a class marker. A mask with professional fit and ventilation bespoke its wearers professional status. A rag of fabric tied crookedly behind the head, by contrast, indicated poverty and desperation. The spring weather had grown almost summer-hot. We passed a young woman understandably parading her pale eight-week-confined flesh in triumphant display, and we noticed she wore more fabric on her face than on the rest of her body. We were randomly selected at a checkpoint to have our temperatures screened before we got on the highway.

Louise and I sat together in the back of my father's car, our faces pressed to opposite windows, our cheeks cooled on the glass. We were avid for landscape, topography, terrain. We held hands across the middle seat like a seventh-grade couple. The scenery dissolved filmically past the window.

(What had happened to Appleton? I never did find out. I searched his name plus *obituary* once and was glad to see that nothing came up. He still lived somewhere; I imagined that he calmly plotted the return, the revenge, of cinema—the people's deliberative art.)

The last time I'd looked at the trees that adjoined the highway, coming back from a Christmas visit to my father, they'd stood bare and skeletal, protesting the winter sky with weak, scraggly arms. Now they shook bouquets of greenery in celebration on the wind. What were they called? I resolved to learn the names of trees, of flowers, of animals.

To enter the suburban borough where I grew up, everyone had their temperatures screened at the border. Cops or doctors —who could tell the difference?—in masks and sunglasses, inscrutable as machines, pointed gauges between our eyes and fired.

When my father pulled into the driveway of the yellow-walled house from the Achilles Shield commercial, Louise whispered, "Hey, I recognize this place."

She fell in love with the library in my father's study. "I could live here," she said one day from the musty futon alongside the desk where she'd been sleeping, where she lay reading his old annotated copy of *The Magic Mountain*. We made love for the first time on that futon—less awkward, we agreed, than in my childhood bedroom—and while it was at times as strange as any novel encounter, we were helped by already knowing each other's bodies in their most frail and wretched state. Everything but sickness and death was then the deepest pleasure.

"I wish I could still live in my library," my father told her at dinner when she repeated for him her praise of his book collection. "But it's all yours. The Agency just sends me TV shows from the streaming services to watch these days, and that takes up all my time."

In that library, on that futon, I wrote these memories of the quarantine. My father has taken an interest in Louise's art and says he may be able to secure her a commission or two and maybe even find a job for me, scholarly as I was—there was still the odd novel or philosophical treatise to be decoded for its potential threat to the nation, and who better to read such texts than myself?

It's been three months since our escape from Brand's building. Louise and I will be married next spring. My father has already asked Dr. Jeong to accompany him to the wedding. Life slowly returns. There's little more to tell, except what follows.

Yesterday, Louise and I drove out to the cemetery where Denise was buried.

"We didn't bring flowers," Louise said aloud to the headstone, "but I bet you weren't a flowers kind of lady anyway." Instead, Louise pulled from her purse an object that fit in the palm of her hand and placed it on top of the marker: a tiny sculpture in paperclips of the figure from *Scraps of Steel* that Denise had touched on the night Louise first showed us her work—the one who waved either in distress or salutation.

"When did you make that?" I asked.

"This morning, while you were in the shower. I got the paperclips from your dad's study drawer. I've decided to only make miniatures from now on—I figure life's too short."

"I don't know if the Agency will agree," I said.

As if she hadn't heard me, she touched her fingers to her belly and said, "All sorts of miniatures."

We laughed, and I took her hand, and we strolled around the empty graveyard for the rest of the afternoon. Its slightly unkempt grass ruffled in the hot early-summer wind as the sunlight drew out its shades of green and gold. Death waited underfoot, and any kind of death might have stalked behind stones and crypts, in the breeze or the trees. Isn't that what the novel virus had taught us? But we were fearless, Louise and I: we had died and come back. We'd earned our citizenship in the land of the deed. We believed we could survive anything else in this life, just as we'd survived the quarantine of St. Sebastian House.

About the Author

John Pistelli was born and raised in Pittsburgh, PA. He now lives in Minneapolis, MN, where he teaches courses in literature and culture. He holds a PhD in English from the University of Minnesota. His short fiction, poetry, reviews, and essays have appeared in many journals, including *Rain Taxi*, *The Millions*, *Five 2 One*, and more. He is the author of the novel *Portraits and Ashes* and the novella *The Ecstasy of Michaela*, and he runs an award-winning literary blog at johnpistelli.com.